CRASH DIVE!

The boat surfaced in a smother of white water
tumbling away as the conning tower broke
free. Wolz led the rush to the bridge and
the guns.

He saw the tall bulky form of the tanker.
And, beyond the tanker's bow, he saw a
betraying flicker of white.

For an instant he stood braced, the Zeiss to
his eyes, staring in passionate anger as the
bows of the destroyer burst into view beyond
and ahead of the tanker.

The destroyer saw them. With a massive
discharge of smoke from her funnel she
slewed hard aport and crashed foaming
headlong towards the U-boat.

'Dive!' bellowed Wolz.

The men on the bridge scurried below. This
time there was no practice about it, no
thought lurking at the back of the mind that
a foul-up would bring only a reprimand.
This time a mistake could cost them all their
lives . . .

Sea Wolf
Steel Shark

BRUNO KRAUSS

SPHERE BOOKS LIMITED
30/32 Gray's Inn Road, London WC1X 8JL

First published in Great Britain by Sphere Books Ltd 1978
Copyright © Bruno Krauss 1978
Reprinted 1978

TRADE
MARK

Set in Linotype Baskerville

Printed in Great Britain by
Hazell Watson & Viney Ltd
Aylesbury, Bucks

CHAPTER ONE

Leutnant zur See Baldur Wolz gripped the Zeiss glasses more firmly and wedged himself even tighter into the corner of the U-boat's conning tower. He stared with deliberate concentration at the distant black rectangle lifting and falling against the horizon rim. Yes. Yes, there could be no mistake.

A fierce exultation seized him. He wanted to shout in violent triumph, to slam his fist against the grey steel of the conning tower. The glasses pressed painfully against his face. He braced himself with the habitual instinctive grace of the born seaman against the U-boat's movement through the sea.

Carefully, repressing all emotion, he lowered the glasses. He was an officer of the most vital arm of the German Navy. Emotion could never be allowed to interfere with his duty. Never.

But if ever a moment for extravagant emotion was to come during the professional career of a U-boat officer, then this very moment had come – now.

'British battleship,' he said, his voice harsh and metallic, ringing clearly over the noise of the sea and the ever-present coughing rumble from the diesels. '*Nelson* or *Rodney*.'

A gleam of sunlight from the watery Atlantic sky shafted down and pulsed brilliantly from his immaculately-combed blond hair. His square, sharp-featured face remained turned towards the fattest target he was ever likely to see. His pale blue-grey eyes regarded with outward equanimity what the gods of war had brought, and, despite all his training and all the rigours through which he had gone, he could not quite control the fierce excitement. He lifted the glasses again to mask the savage look of expectation that, for

5

only an instant, turned his face from that of a pleasant – even a handsome – young German into that of a savage killer.

No mistake. A battleship. That enormous block of steel lifting high above the low decks, the suggestion of that long forecastle with its three massive turrets, yes, that was *Nelson* or *Rodney*, without a doubt. A British battleship. The greatest prize.

Kapitanleutnant Gustav Ludecke, U-42's Commander, although sharing all the bubbling excitement of his Second Officer, carried that special responsibility conferred on a man by command at sea. 'Hands to diving stations.' Ludecke spoke calmly. 'She's on a collision course. The English evidently wish to throw themselves into our jaws.' He laughed, then, because the emotions of the moment had to find some outlet.

Low down, low and lean, the U-boat slid through the waves like a lean and hungry wolf. High up in their massive steel superstructure the English look-outs would never spot the boat before the torpedoes crunched sickeningly in. Against the lighter sky, surface ships stood out like targets in a shooting gallery.

All the same, Ludecke was taking no chances.

Course corrections were plotted and read off, the conning tower was cleared of all save the Commander and the Second Officer. Then, as the battleship ploughed grandly on, since the presence of her two escorting destroyers must be evaluated and considered, Ludecke turned to Wolz.

'Below with you, Baldur.' Then, with strict naval discipline: 'Periscope depth.'

Dropping through the conning tower Wolz realized once again that however extrovert and brash his commanding officer might be, however daredevil an appearance he presented, he was in sober reality a most experienced and cautious commander. The British battleship's course, for all her changes, would bring her down onto U-42. There was no need for the watch to tumble madly down, each man allowed one and one-fifth seconds, and for the hatch to be slammed in all haste. Ludecke had brought his boat to diving readiness and now he took her down to fourteen metres gently, without a great spouting of white water, smoothly. Like a vicious shark she slid beneath the surface of the sea, ready and waiting.

The marked difference in sensations pouring in to the crew told each veteran exactly what was happening, second by second. The thunderous bellow of the diesels ceased. Then came the clack of the hatch shutting, the hissing roar of compressed air. The table lights blinked on, each one shining confidently, assurance that the tanks were flooding in order, for'ard to aft, the aftermost tank left until the end. The electric motors took up their task with that almost inaudible thrilling, a sensation felt more through the soles of the feet than through the ears.

At fourteen metres the U-boat slid through the water, lean and grey and deadly.

'Up periscope!'

Ludecke grasped the handles and lifted as the tube slid up. Although his cap with its battered peak was no hindrance, he habitually turned it around so the peak jutted aft when he took observations through the periscope. This was just one of those little touches about the man that endeared him to his crew. A just man, a firm commander, a fine professional U-boat fighter, Gustav Ludecke had been training men for the U-boat service from the beginning of the Kriegsmarine's rebirth. And now, on his very first operational cruise, he was being presented with the very finest target of all.

Exactly two months ago Gunther Prien in U-47 had penetrated the defences of Scapa Flow and sunk *Royal Oak*. For all the tremendous fuss that had been made – rightfully for so daring a deed – Ludecke knew that *Royal Oak* was an old and obsolescent battleship.

Nelson and *Rodney* were both much more important units. To send one of those to the bottom! Ludecke could well imagine the kind of celebrations *that* would bring.

The two destroyers must still be there – the hydrophone operator was sending in his reports with regularity – but Ludecke could see only one of them, foaming along, cutting across on the starboard bow of the battleship. He took a long last look and then snapped: 'Down periscope!'

'A fine fat target, gentlemen,' he said.

Gunther Meisten, the First Officer, said: 'A fine fat present for the Fuhrer.'

Baldur Wolz, busy attending to duties drilled and re-drilled into him, was perfectly able to appreciate the Commander's reaction, and to feel a peculiar mixture of anger, despair, and anxiety.

For Gustav Ludecke laughed, filled with the promise of the supreme triumph to come, and most offhandedly said: 'Had the Fuhrer been a sailor instead of a soldier, the German Navy could win this war in a couple of weeks. As he was not – we must do what we can with what he has so kindly allowed us.'

Oberleutnant zur See Meisten bristled up. He was a lean man, harsh-featured, very exact in every detail and a member of the Party. Wolz could see the lumps ridge along his jaw. The dedication he gave to the Fuhrer and the Party was not shared by the Commander, and Wolz was darkly aware that Ludecke, in not giving a damn, relying on the good old German naval traditions, was running headlong into dangers that might only be half-seen, half-sensed, but were profoundly deadly for all that.

About to spit out an acid comment, Meisten was interrupted by Ludecke's cheerful: 'Up periscope!'

As the tube slid up Ludecke swung the lenses in a full three hundred and sixty degree sweep.

'We have him all to ourselves,' Ludecke said, and as

8

the tube came down he laughed again. Well, if ever there was a time to laugh, this was it. Or, reflected Wolz with that same deadly quality he had displayed during all the training sessions in the Baltic, or, better yet, the time to laugh would be when the English battleship sank gurgling into the sea.

All those months of training would pay off now. Wolz had fought his way through naval training with the dogged persistence of a starving wolf on the trail, determined to beat and overcome all the service obstacles. His father had sunk in his U-boat right at the end of the last war, rammed by a damned careless German minesweeper. So Wolz, reared by an aunt in some comfort, had very good reasons for becoming a U-boat man and for taming and beating all the sea, the enemy and the U-boats themselves could do against him.

The comforting array of dials and switches, valves and pipes, every one of which he knew like an old friend, assured him that if technical competence counted, then the battleship was theirs already. Claustrophobia barred off those sailors who were not U-boat men. Wolz, in his element, fully trained, determined, motivated, understood the U-boat as an expert rider understands his horse.

But, of course, there was always the unexpected. No one ever took liberties with a submarine. One mistake and the water would flood in and the hull would crumple under the ferocious pressures of the depths, and that would be that.

'Up periscope!'

Ludecke rattled off the course and bearings, sharp, in command, knowing exactly what he was doing. Now only the Commander could see what was happening on the surface. Only he could see the sunlight and the waves. Everyone else was locked into the narrow steel tube of the pressure hull, confined in the grey steel walls of the U-boat, mentally as well as physically.

The plots were laid down nicely, the table chunked out the answers, the boat glided gently on. Wolz knew the moment was fast approaching.

Tension gripped them all. The air with its familiar ever-present aromas of oil and pitch and sea water and the faint lingering aftertaste of cabbage, reassured a U-boat man, though Wolz had known tough sailors of the surface fleet to gag and momentarily flinch back as they set foot on the conning tower and caught that exciting smell wafting up.

Ludecke gave his orders in a calm, firm voice, bringing his boat around, waiting until exactly the right moment to shoot. The torpedo room forward was closed up, every man knowing exactly what to do and ready to leap into instant action the moment the command was given.

Once more the Commander ordered down periscope. Wolz took a breath. The plots showed the story. The next time the attacking scope would bring up the battleship, big and powerful, shouldering through the seas, and the cross wires would come on, and then ... then ... Baldur Wolz's hands gripped into fists. One day, God and the Fuhrer – and Befehlshaber des Unterseeboote, the U-boat High Command – willing, he would command his own boat. Then he would give the orders. Then it would be his brain and skill pitted against the enemy.

As it was he watched his gauges and kept right on top of his duty and sweated out this time of stalking like all the others.

During a submerged attack the Commander always controlled everything himself. Only he saw the target. He read off the course and the ranges, so that his orders through the chain of command at last reached the Torpedo man at the forward tubes, whose duty was to make sure the fish really did leave the tubes.

After what seemed an interminable wait, Ludecke drew a breath and, firmly, gave the final order.

'*Loose!*'

The familiar heavy thump through the boat ... The hiss of compressed air ... The flurry as the Chief flooded to compensate for the discharged torpedo ...

'*Loose!*'

Again the hiss and the thump, the feel of being in action, and yet all the time the U-boat glided beneath the surface of the sea, unseen, unsuspected, lean and deadly ...

Four torpedoes sped unerringly for the sheer steel side of the British battleship.

Oberleutnant Meisten began counting.

Wolz, too, counted beneath his breath.

They waited.

The harsh white light beat upon their faces, shadowed with stubble. Their eyes caught the light and gleamed whitely. No-one moved. A stasis of hungry expectation held them all rigid, waiting ...

The boat slid deeper into the sea, away from the expected vicious reaction from the escorting destroyers.

Still Meisten counted.

Ludecke looked at the First Lieutenant and his face expressed the feelings of a man chewing filth.

Still Meisten counted.

A report from the hydrophone operator: 'Sir! Two heavy thuds – propeller noises steady – no change—'

'Damn! Damn! Damn!' bellowed Ludecke. He snatched off his white submariner's cap and threw it to the steel deck plating.

'The fish hit!' he shouted, red-faced, sweating, ugly. 'The eels hit – and they did not explode!'

He swung back. 'Any change in the destroyers' propellers?'

'No change, sir,' sang out the hydrophone operator. 'Steady on course—'

'Bring her up to fourteen metres,' snapped Ludecke.

The U-boat's saddle tanks hissed with compressed air and the water boiled out. She lifted through the green depths, rising up to periscope depth.

'Up periscope!'

Ludecke grasped the handles, twisting the left hand grip with accustomed ease to compensate for the boat's motion. He swung the scope through three hundred and sixty degrees. With his right hand he adjusted the angle of sight, giving the sky a clear scan. Not that scouting aircraft were likely, here in the South Atlantic, but U-boatmen stayed alive by being careful. Wolz, with all the others, waited.

At last Ludecke ordered down periscope. He took his cap from the proffered hand of Meisten. His face looked like that of a savage bull tormented and goaded, ready to leap out and gore anyone who approached, but held fast by thick iron chains.

'Well, gentlemen. They are gone. A fine battleship – *Rodney*, for sure – a perfectly executed attack, two hits – and what do we have to show for it all?'

He stared about at his officers.

'Nothing, gentlemen. Nothing. Four fish wasted. We might as well have stayed at home in Kiel.'

'Not quite, sir,' said Meisten, formally. 'We still have *Graf Spee* to—'

'Quite, Herr Oberleutnant. Quite! I do not think I need you to remind me of my duty. Resume course and speed.' Ludecke was behaving, Wolz considered, in a most controlled way. By God! If that happened to him when he was in command! It was horrific. Ludecke glared about. 'I shall require a full report on the status of every torpedo aboard. Every one. I want to know why when I hit my target some damn fool fouls me up! I want to know why the torpedoes did not explode! If I find some idiot has made a stupid mistake, I'll have his insides spread all over the chart table and personally dissect them with the bluntest knife and fork I can find!'

And with this Kapitanleutnant Gustav Ludecke barged off to the wardroom and his captain's cabin curtained off in one corner. Somehow any thoughts of pity for the Commander in Baldur Wolz's mind were tinged with an unidentifiable apprehension for the future. This technical failure seemed to him to be intimately wrapped up with a personal failure.

CHAPTER TWO

The long undulating motion of the waves broke creaming away from the sharp prow of the U-boat, ran in smothering surges past her lean flanks. The rounded casings of the ballast tanks could not detract from the impression of immense controlled power. Baldur Wolz, leaning on the coaming of the conning tower, looked at the water creaming away from for'ard, slapping at the long deck casing. Bright early morning sunlight caught the water, glittering. Life was good, at sea, with all the ocean to hunt in, with a grey wolf to drive, with fat targets to seek and destroy.

He looked around the horizon. The seaman on watch, Speidel, a good hand, stared also, quartering the horizon. The signalman stood ready to handle his duties as well as to keep watch. Good U-boatmen had to be able to do more than just handle the duties connected with their own department.

Wolz glanced at his wrist watch. No point now in asking for more coffee. He would be off watch in ten minutes, when Leutnant zur See Willi Weidman would relieve him, and then he might drink the stuff in greater comfort. The weather remained fine and clear, with a gentle sea and no wind to speak of. Only a few clouds cut off the glare. They were drawing nearer and nearer to the coast of South America, and whatever adventures might befall them there.

He reflected that if this had been a peaceful cruise before the war nothing would have been lacking – save the presence of some pretty girls to make the picture complete. Baldur Wolz liked girls. As a personable young man of twenty-one, his birthday having been spent riotously on the eleventh of November, he had found no difficulty in actually having girls speak to him and be willing to be seen in his company. The problems usually started when he began to grow a little warmer with them.

Now that Lottie, for instance, with the organdie dress of some indescribable flame colour, and silk stockings encasing slender legs that had flashed with blood-thumping enragement when he'd chased her down the main staircase, to catch her about the waist and fall in a tumbled heap on the carpet at the foot – somehow he'd found his hands filled with the softness of her breasts, somehow she was biting his ear, somehow his hands were no longer outside that organdie dress but inside it through the barriers of press-studs and buttons – somehow she was startlingly red of face, and gasping, and he was running his hands frenziedly over her body, feeling her skin warm, warm – and somehow they were in his uncle's study with the swastika flags and the portraits of the Fuhrer and the bronze busts and they were rolling under the massive polished desk and all the buttons burst and so she lifted up, gasping, her body bare and flaunting from the waist, rising up from the flame organdie, and he was seizing her and dragging her down, his hands filled with soft beauty and his mouth against hers, warm and moist and alive, and—

A wave slapped the steel hull and ran along in a combing crest, to splatter him with warm drops of water.

Well, Lottie had been moist and soft and sweet, and he'd thoroughly enjoyed it, even if the silk stockings had been laddered so badly she had made him buy her a dozen new pairs. Her silk camiknickers had proved no obstacle to a tough U-boat man. Well, reflected Wolz, wiping the water from his eyes, well, on his very next leave Lottie might ask for two dozen pairs of silk stockings – if they were to be had he would get them, for she had a way with her, squirming and sighing and wriggling and clasping him, that he found highly enjoyable.

The way those buttons had sprayed across the carpet!

Just as well his uncle had been away in Berlin about his duties, and his aunt peacefully sleeping off the effects of her early mild invasion of the party.

His aunt and uncle had been good to him, taking him in when his mother died soon after his father had gone to the bottom in the tangled and crushed hull of his U-boat.

Luckily enough Lottie was rich enough to afford her own transport – her father having a finger in more than one factory manufacturing armaments – and so she was spared the raucous comments of the survivors of the party. Young people about to enter upon a war they all instinctively felt would be the great justification of all their hopes, they fully intended to live life to the hilt. Drink, women, fast cars, near-insane gambling, these drove that charmed circle. Baldur Wolz, because naval training had taken him further away than most, could afford to look on, a part of and yet a little removed from the charmed circle.

Sharp on eight bells Willi Weidman came on deck, looking decidedly unhappy. A thin, elegant young man, he had gone through the Hitler Youth, which Wolz had avoided through naval duty, and yet he still retained enough foolishness to accept Wolz's invitation and to fit in splendidly with the fast set centred around Wolz's cousins.

Giving the course and making a few general observations, Wolz firmly refused to think about his cousins, and, in particular, about Lisl. Tumbling Lottie was almost a game, a pastime, something he had done because it seemed to be the thing to do – and, anyway, because Lottie was young and fresh and sweet and panting for it. But to think of treating Lisl in that way ... No. No, that was something entirely different.

16

'Daddy's in a most frightful temper this morning,' observed Willi, morosely. 'No one could find a damned thing wrong with the tinfish.'

'I know. But they failed to explode. That was *Rodney* we missed. No wonder Daddy's hopping mad.'

'Tread with great care, Baldur. I wouldn't put it past Daddy to masthead anyone up the periscope, the mood he's in.'

Wolz smiled. Willi liked a dramatic turn of phrase from time to time. It gave him, he would say with a confidential look and ill-mannered leer, an air of being an old sea salt, with a hundred thousand tons in the locker.

Willi had emerged after Wolz's party with his clothes wildly disarrayed, a champagne bottle clutched to his bosom, his fly buttons missing, and a red-head and a brunette clutching his arms and shrieking for their next sip of champagne. What had been going on in other parts of the schloss Wolz had no need to enquire. Just so long as they'd all enjoyed themselves.

With a last mocking word to the effect that Willi had better not report any albatrosses as Sunderlands, or whales as enemy submarines, Wolz slid down the ladder to the inner hatch and then to the control room. He jumped to the deck and turned, ready to head into the wardroom for his coffee.

The sound of sparks flying came from the radio room directly opposite the commander's cabin.

Every day the U-boat must report her position and then listen out for orders from BdU. Donitz of BdU, kept an iron grip on all his boats, and most of the submarine commanders took comfort from this, aware that their movements were being watched over and their welfare considered. The best BdU could do was put them squarely in the path of heavy tonnages. Wolz drank his coffee down, making only a little grimace – coffee as a drink rated far too high in the Navy and that thick British cocoa the English called kai which he had sampled during a visit was something he wished the German Navy had copied from the Royal Navy along with everything else – and put the cup down carefully. Well, BdU had known nothing of *Rodney*. They knew now, though, from the Kapitanleutnant's report. No doubt Ludecke had been bitterly scathing in the best professional way over the malfunction of the torpedoes.

General opinion inclined to the belief that the trouble lay with the magnetic pistols. Torpedoes were designed to run deep and pass under the enemy ship, when the steel plating would trigger the magnetic pistol, detonate the explosive warhead, and stove in the bottom plating of the ship, which was her most vulnerable point.

Kapitanleutnant Ludecke appeared in the wardroom, looking grim. The harsh lighting emphasised the stubble on his chin, and also the hard light in his eyes. He held a message flimsy. By the time elapsed since the message had been received and the quietness from the commander's cabin, Wolz guessed the signal to be Commander's Cipher. Ordinary code messages were handled at once; cipher messages had to have a special setting on the coding machine. For Commander's Cipher signals the machine must be set again, this time in a key held only by the U-boat commander.

Meisten looked up and both he and Wolz stood up as Ludecke scowled at them.

'Well, gentlemen, our mission has been terminated.'

Without further explanation Ludecke went through to the control room and gave the necessary orders that brought the boat from her course of two-oh-eight around to eighty.

Wolz looked at Meisten. The First Officer in his punctilious way had never yet overly annoyed Wolz, although he took a delight in riding his subordinates. Wolz was used to that. It had formed part of his training in the sailing flotilla in the Baltic and at the

Academy. He had noticed that whereas the old salts would bellow and curse and seek to put their pupils through hell, the whole process was done in the full knowledge that it was part of a tradition, and the way to turn out first class sailors. The officers who belonged to the party, Wolz had found out, had a somewhat different attitude to discipline. Sometimes Meisten's domineering and even brutal methods made Wolz reflect that the First Officer's absence from the Hitler Youth and the Party's roll-musters was not altogether a bad thing.

Now Meisten said: 'What's happened now? It was by special order of the Fuhrer that we were to support *Graf Spee*.'

Coming back into the wardroom, Ludecke heard him. His lips set firmly. His usually reckless attitude had stiffened, so that he looked angry and purposeful. The moment he spoke Wolz understood what had happened.

'Now we know why *Rodney* was on a reciprocal course. I have just had distressing news. *Graf Spee* has been sunk in action, a glorious end for a great fighting ship.'

Wolz felt the keen stab of dismay. A pocket battleship, able to outgun anything that could catch her, and outrun anything that could outgun her – sunk! Only three ships' could have done that – *Hood*, *Renown* or *Repulse*, for they had the speed and the gunpower.

Meisten looked outraged. He thumped a fist angrily onto the table. 'Who was it, sir, *Hood*?'

'The signal does not specify, Herr Oberleutnant. But whoever it was – *Graf Spee* has gone, and our mission of support no longer has meaning. We are to resume our cruise with special regard to the Freetown area.'

That made sense. Having been dragged so far out into the Atlantic on an abnormally long patrol, the boat should logically be used to create havoc where she would not be expected and where escorts could be assumed to be weak.

'This cruise can be turned into a profitable one,' said Ludecke. 'Had we been a type II boat we would never have got beyond coastal waters. As it is, being a type IX, we are naturally selected for long-range patrols – and are naturally expected to turn in correspondingly better results.' He looked at his officers with a fierce, down-drawn look. 'I shall engage any runners on the surface. Until I am certain of the torpedoes I prefer to trust to shellfire.'

Again, that made sense.

The type IX's carried one 10.5 centimetre, one 3.7 centimetre and a 2.0 centimetre flak gun. With that kind of armament, handled by professional Navy sailors, they could destroy any normal freighter they might encounter, even if it was equipped with the obsolete and slow six-inch guns mounted in British merchant ships.

'Herr Leutnant Wolz,' snapped Ludecke, formally. 'You will personally check every pistol and make sure each is functioning perfectly. Nothing has been found at fault. I want you to double-check.' Some of the frustration at his ill-luck boiled up in the Commander as he added: 'When I use the eels next time I want to be sure they will work.'

'Yes, sir,' said Wolz. 'I understand.'

'Make it so.'

Just before he began his task, for discipline required he obey at once and to hell with any ideas of sleep, Wolz turned as Meisten called after him, low enough not to be overheard.

'Just imagine it's a girl's legs you're inspecting, Wolz. That way you'll be able to keep your mind on your task.'

'Yes, sir,' said Wolz, going out, not caring to make any further reply.

But, by God, wasn't the insufferable fellow right!

The Engineer Officer, Helmut Bergmann, going aft to crouch over his beloved engines and handle them with doting affection and furious antipathy, according to their behaviour, could muster only a mumbled: 'Bad news about *Graf Spee*, Baldur.'

There was nothing that Wolz, in all decency, could say. Losses must be expected in war. Any comment on sacrifices to be made was adequately dealt with by all those gold-leaf-bedecked high officers every time they addressed a parade.

Wolz pushed past the bulkhead, ducking, and looked for'ard into the torpedo compartment. The men's bunks were pushed up out of the way. White paint, the glare of white lighting, miles of white piping running along the hull – the place gleamed and glittered like an operating theatre. The torpedoes gleamed with polish. The reloads had been loaded into the tubes and Wolz decided to deal with those first, drawing one fish at a time. The operation was not overly tricky if the drill was followed. He set about his task philosophically, the torpedo-men obeying him with the alacrity to be expected and, also because they understood that this smart young officer knew his job.

Every U-boat man knew his job – months of incessant training saw to that – but out of all those keen and dedicated young men some stood forth as exemplars. Foremost among the commanders at this time, thought Wolz, must surely stand Gunther Prien of U-47. One day, one day, Baldur Wolz would command his own boat and conn her to victory.

As it was, he must sweat over these damned magnetic pistols, tearing into the tinfish as though each one was a personal obstacle to be overcome. The type IX's carried four tubes for'ard and two aft, and the boats had been designed for extended ocean raiding. The tropical conditions were trying, and the men sweated and grumbled in best naval style, but the boats were good and the men were good. It now remained for Kapitanleutnant Gustav Ludecke to be dealt a good hand in the luck game, without which no U-boat commander could achieve anything.

Here in the open sea they were pounding along at twelve knots to reach the thronged shipping lanes. Once astride these vital arteries of commerce the U-boat could begin the task for which she had been designed.

Up in the conning tower Leutnant zur See Willi Weidman clamped the Zeiss glasses to his eyes and scanned the horizon.

A thin smear, like a random chalk mark, stained the distant sky above the horizon rim. Weidman looked carefully. He shut his eyes and peered again. Then he lowered the glasses and shouted down into the U-boat.

'Smoke! Bearing Green oh-seven-oh.'

At once U-42 sprang into purposeful life.

CHAPTER THREE

With every man at his post, with the diesels running sweetly and bringing the boat swiftly up to fourteen, sixteen, seventeen knots, U-42 raced across the sparkling waters. Ludecke gave course corrections, aiming his boat well ahead of the course of the distant steamer so that the point of intersection would be reached in the shortest possible time.

Look-outs continually scanned the sky. For all Wolz's light-hearted chaffing of Willi Weidman and the constant sky search, no-one really believed the English would have put patrol aircraft out at this distance. The African coast lay miles away. This steamer must have taken the run around the Cape and was plugging away for home confident that her speed would enable her to elude the slinking U-boats.

Well, the English had miscalculated.

Kapitanleutnant Ludecke was determined to put this fine fat freighter where she belonged, at the bottom of the ocean.

Soon the upperworks of the ship hove into view. A tall square funnel, three masts, the smallness of the bridge always surprising. They'd probably have an old six-inch gun mounted on the fantail. That had to be taken into consideration.

His naturally optimistic, flamboyant personality responded to the challenge. Ludecke itched to get the freighter in his sights. He'd use the 10.5 centimetre gun, blow a few holes in the ship, show these damned arrogant English who controlled the seas now!

'She's doing a good twelve knots, sir,' said Weidman.

Ludecke nodded without replying. She was a fast

runner and he'd have to catch her on the surface. To dive now would be useless.

'Gun's crew close up,' he said when the freighter's next expected change of course did not take place. She had put her stern on to the U-boat. A flicker of white grew more strongly at her stern. Huge clouds of black smoke rose from that square funnel.

'Meisten!' snapped Ludecke. 'Put a shot across her!'

The men at the gun moved with instinctive reactions to the surge of the boat. Spray flew back. Meisten wiped the sights, having checked that the watertight sealing of the gun had been removed. A moment's delay, then with a sharp and defiant crack, the gun fired.

The smoke slashed back across the deck.

Ludecke peered carefully at the fleeing ship. He was catching her. He could see no sign of the fall of shot. He bent to the voicepipe. 'Ease her, Chief. Fifteen knots.'

The motion of the U-boat eased perceptibly. 'Try again, Number One.'

Again the gun barked. This time they could all see the white splash and the climbing fountain of water. Over and to the right.

The signaller shouted: 'Signal to Commander. Enemy radioing S.O.S.'

'Damn!' said Ludecke. 'Number One! Put a brick into his radio shack. Hit the beggar on the bridge!'

This time Meisten licked his lips as he bent to the gun.

The smash of the discharge and the gush of smoke had to be disregarded. Anxiously, they all gazed at the ship.

A bright flash of flame high on the superstructure. Bits and pieces flying up, black against the sunglare ...

'And again!'

The gun rapped out angrily once more. Another hit.

Then, with the unexpectedness of a stage trapdoor devil, the gun mounted on the freighter's stern belched a livid line of fire, a cloud of smoke. A white spout erupted in the sea five hundred metres to port and well over.

A runner clanged up the iron ladder, bringing the intercepted message.

Ludecke gave an order before glancing at the slip.

'Five rounds rapid! Knock his radio shack to pieces!'

The message read: 'Under attack from German submarine. Urgently require assistance.' The position given corresponded with that recorded earlier by Ludecke. A long string of S.S.S., S.S.S. followed.

'Is he still signalling?'

'Yes, sir—' The signaller paused and then, looking up, shouted: 'Transmissions ceased, sir!'

Looking across the narrowing strip of water Ludecke saw the mass of brown smoke rolling from the bridge of the freighter He chuckled.

'That's stopped his little game!'

The six-incher from the poop fired again.

'Number One! Put three rounds about those fellows' ears!'

Meisten enjoyed his work. His 10.5 centimetre spat three times. Everyone gave a cheer when the bright flash from the stern of the freighter brought an abrupt end to the shooting.

'He's stopping, sir! Lowering boats.'

'Good.'

The boat-handling of the British freighter brought a growl of approval from Ludecke. 'Those fellows are pretty sharp about it.'

Meisten laughed. 'A few shells up their backsides, sir! That's enough to make them scurry like the rats they are.'

'Rats they may be, but their ship is not sinking yet.'

Ludecke eased his boat and brought her around easily in the sea. The boats from the freighter wallowed off, most of the oars pulled in unison. The men in the boats looked small and fragile. The sea slapped the casing of the U-boat in the aimless way of the water when forward motion ceased.

Now, as the U-boat watched from her position a thousand metres off, Ludecke hauled her slowly forward again, closing gently. By peering past the slab of the conning tower Wolz, standing gripping the rail of the wintergarden, could see the ship. The massive brown smear of smoke appeared to be lessening. He could see no flames from the bridge. No-one could be seen on the fantail and the six-inch gun poked out, like a dead tree-branch, useless.

Yes, Wolz conceded, Meisten had done fine shooting. Some vague prickle of unease stirred the delicate professional tendrils of Baldur Wolz, but he ignored his instincts. Ludecke was a first rate commander; the First Lieutenant knew his job. Between them they had brought this ship to a halt, seen the crew off, and now all that remained was to finish the ship off by shellfire and send her to the bottom.

The 3.7 centimetre gun, ready-loaded, fully-manned, would not be used in this action. Ludecke would give the order to Meisten, the big 10.5 centimetre piece would punch a few shellholes along the waterline, and U-42 could chalk up her first kill.

The inevitability of it all brought a sense of fitness to Baldur Wolz. This was how submarine warfare should be carried out. He stared at the English boats as Ludecke brought U-42 around further, heading for the cluster. Yes, eminently satisfying.

Captain E. J. Hammon, master of S.S. *Willowmore*, coughed a great gob of spittle from his inflamed lungs. He spat overboard, almost retching. His bright bandanna wiped his streaming eyes. The filthy brown smoke clung about him on the shambles of his bridge. At his back poor Williams had gone on sending from the radio shack until a direct hit from the U-boat's

26

forward gun had blasted shack, radio and Williams to perdition.

Hammon just hoped the distress call had been picked up. A destroyer might be sent. Whatever happened to that damned U-boat out there, whether the destroyer found her and sunk her or not, all that would be when the S.S. *Willowmore* lay rusting away on the bottom of the sea.

He looked over the ruined bridge and saw the bloody mess through the hole in the shelter deck that was all that was left of his First Officer, Andrews. Andrews had been shaping up, a fine seaman, and now some godforsaken German in a tin submarine had blown him to a bloody pulp.

Hammon coughed again, spitting, and turned as the Bos'n climbed onto the bridge.

'Boats away, sir.' The Bos'n eyed him, his eyes white and maniacal in his blackened face. His shirt was ripped across and blood dripped from his shoulder. 'You coming, sir?'

'Who's left aboard, Bos'n?'

'You an' me, sir, and the last boat's crew. Mister Davids has 'em holding on—'

Hammon made up his mind. He stared again across the water at the low ominous shape of the U-boat now creeping towards the huddle of boats. Those eyes of E. J. Hammon – bleak and bitter – stared with hunger at the shape of the U-boat.

'Bos'n,' he said, almost dreamily, 'Bos'n – did you know I went to sea in '16 as a youngster in a Special Services craft?'

'Aye, sir. Q-ships, that's what they was.' The Bos'n followed his captain's gaze. 'He's getting ready to sink us, sir—'

'Our panic party went over in fine style, Bos'n. Tell Mister Davids I want three men aft. The six-inch is still in firing condition. That bastard out there only killed the crew. Tell—'

'Aye aye, sir!' The Bos'n, big and bluff and bleeding from the shoulder, did not need to be told in detail. 'We'll sink the bugger, sir—'

'If we do not, he will sink us – and if we meekly let him take us off, he'll still sink us. I'd rather like to get my whack at a U-boat.' He smiled, then, the bitterness deflected after twenty-one years. 'I never saw a damned German U-boat at all – the last time.'

'Aye aye, sir.'

The Bos'n leapt away. Captain E. J. Hammon, Master of the nine thousand four hundred ton dead-weight freighter, *Willowmore*, from Cape Town to Liverpool, went carefully through the shambles of his ship towards the aft six-inch gun.

Perhaps, this time, he would get himself a sub ...

Kapitanleutnant Ludecke leaned over the coaming of his conning tower.

'Weidman – go forward. Keep your side-arms handy. Don't let the Englishmen get aboard.' He turned to speak directly to Meisten. 'Herr Oberleutnant. You will oblige me by placing four shots into the freighter's waterline and sinking her.'

'Very good, sir!'

Meisten checked the gunlaying and stepped back. The long black muzzle pointed at the waterline. In seconds a shell would smash into the thin plating and the waters of the Atlantic would roar in.

'Fire!'

With an ear-splitting crash the gun bellowed, chunks of metal flew, a man shrieked and span backwards, to slither and slide off the casing and plummet into the sea.

Ludecke yelled in anger. Meisten was holding his head. Bright blood ran through his fingers.

Smoke wafted back. Wolz sprang up from the win-tergarden to glare at the Captain.

'Those damned English!' shouted Ludecke.

From the stern of the British freighter a white puff of smoke drifted away.

'They've re-opened fire – hit on the gun as it fired – damned close shave.' He bellowed down to Meisten. 'Can you shoot, Number One?'

Meisten staggered up. His face looked ghastly.

'No, sir.'

'Damn, damn, damn!' bellowed Ludecke. His words were cut off by another crack from the six-inch. This time the shot plunged into the sea. Sailors were throwing lines to the man in the water. Blood spread around him and he sank from view. It was Hans Liederbecke, a man from Bremen, who always had a laugh and a joke even in the trickiest situations.

Wolz disregarded all that. Another report from the English ship and a shell plummeted down to send up a spout of water that drenched the conning tower. Baldur Wolz leaped down from the conning tower to the wintergarden aft and bellowed at his gun crew.

'Stand to! Target gun on English ship. Eight hundred metres. *Fire!*'

The 3.7 centimetre cracked out, a whiplash of vicious sound amid the deeper concussions of the bigger guns.

The gunner loaded with desperate haste. Wolz kept the gun in action, kept the shells pumping out. He saw bright flashes on the hull.

'Up! Elevation! Jump to it!'

Now the shell-strikes flowered along the stern. He saw the dark figures of men working frantically at the gun, saw the flash, the bright lick of flame, saw the men staggering back.

'Keep shooting!'

The clang of the breech, the scrape of metal, the bitter taste of cordite, the smash and concussion of discharge, the ring of the shell cases on the steel deck ... Staring with that fierce hunting look on his face Wolz saw the last of the British gun crew fall. The gun stood, alone, silent, finished.

'Cease fire!'

Ludecke peered over the side.

'Well done!'

He swung back.

'Secure guns. Everyone below.' The ship had sent out an S.O.S. He could not delay. Every minute brought the chance of a destroyer appearing over the horizon, foaming along at thirty knots, asdic and depth-charges at the ready. 'Diving stations. Periscope depth. Take her down!'

Wolz tumbled below, his feet loud on the iron rungs. The crew vanished into the pressure hull to take up their positions. Everything had happened so fast he was still gripped in the fever of firing his gun, of see-ing the shells bursting on the Englishman's gun, of feeling the tremendous elation of victory.

The clang of the hatch shutting brought him back to reality.

Ludecke's booted feet appeared. He span the wheel to lock the hatch and then dropped down.

The flooding water gushed into the tanks and the boat tilted. Down to periscope depth with the needles flickering across the gauges, the sound of the electric motors taking over from the diesels, the sensation of once more being underwater, in the true element of the boat, calmed everyone down.

'Up periscope!'

Walther Bohm hauled on the lever and the tube slid up. Ludecke grasped the handles, pulling them down as they lifted with the rise of the scope. He jammed his face into the rubber eyepiece and stared hungrily at the English ship.

'Ten thousand tons, for a certainty. On the Cape Town run. *Willowmore*. Her name was large enough. Well, the bastard, I'll have to waste a fish on her. And pray to God the magnetic pistol works.'

He called off the range and depth. Dead in the water after her final run with engines stopped, *Willowmore* simply wallowed in the sea, a stationary target ... He could not miss. If the eel did not explode ... Well, he would not think of that now.

'Loose!'

The fish hissed and thumped and the boat shook and the Chief flooded to compensate, all the familiar sounds remarked on and stored away and not noticed unless they were different from the expected ...

Still watching through the scope Ludecke saw the abrupt spout of white water alongside *Willowmore*. The hydrophone operator yelled. But everyone heard that deep glorious booming roar through the water.

A bedlam of shouting and cheering broke out.

Ludecke slapped the 'scope handles up and Bohm flicked the tube down.

'Silence! Silence, you pack of undisciplined rabble-mongers! This is a U-boat, not some poxy whore-house! Silence!'

The noise died away.

But the faces of the men showed what they felt.

U-42 had opened her score.

And that, reflected Baldur Wolz as U-42 slipped away to resume her cruise, was worth a cheer or two.

CHAPTER FOUR

The enquiry was carried out with the utmost rigour but in the end it all came down to a positive statement by Meisten and the gun crew that Hans Leiderbecke had been dead before he hit the water. A shell fragment had ripped out his guts and chest, exposing his heart and lungs, and no-one was going to recover from injuries like that.

Willi Weidman's party, seeing Liederbecke in the water, had thrown lines, not realising the man was dead.

U-42 drove steadily northwards, at eight knots, her look-outs eternally searching for the next *Willowmore*.

Meisten's attitude further displeased Baldur Wolz.

'We should have machine-gunned the bastards,' he said, venomously, fingering the plaster covering the wound on his face. He'd have a scar there, and not from a sabre. 'They had surrendered and then re-opened fire. They all deserve to hang.'

Mildly, Wolz said: 'The flag was still flying, sir – the Red Ensign had not been pulled down, and—'

'Are you arguing with me, Leutnant? When they take to the boats, isn't that to say the fight's over?'

Wolz bit back what he was going to say: what fight?

Instead, he said: 'With all respect, sir, I do not think you can fault a man for fighting until he is killed '

'The English have no sense in these matters.' Here Meisten must have realised he sounded like a fool, for he added with cutting sarcasm: 'I understand you spent some time in England, before the war. Perhaps the English have tarred you with some of the same brush.'

Luckily for Wolz – very luckily – the Commander

stepped into the wardroom and so the subject of the conversation changed at once to technical matters.

'Get the water wagtail up. You can fly her, Baldur. Willi can have his chance next.'

At their expressions Ludecke realised something had been troubling them, and he misconstrued the argument, wrapped up in his own anxieties.

'It's no good worrying about what is past. Liederbecke is dead and gone. Roses do not flower on a sailor's grave. Now, Baldur, we are coming into the thickest part of the sailing lanes. We shall sight a nice fat freighter and send her to the bottom.'

Meisten recovered quickly.

'Yes, sir. But the gun is useless. And the 3.7 won't do the work satisfactorily, so—'

'Quite, Herr Oberleutnant, quite.'

Wolz took a little satisfaction from the Commander's tone. Meisten was becoming unbearable. The insufferable nerve of the fellow to make even a glancing suggestion that Wolz's time in England might have made him soft! Going out through the conning tower and rousing the hands responsible for the two big cylinders containing the kite he decided he would have to think hard about what to do with this jumped-up Meisten.

His uncle, a strong Party man because, as Wolz had decided with the cheerful cynicism of youth, that brought him fat contracts from the Luftwaffe and the Wehrmacht, had once confided in Baldur to a surprising degree. Of course, Uncle Siegfried had been more than a trifle drunk at the time, the expensive French champagne on which he doted and with which he amply stocked the cellars of the schloss having given him the rubicund, cheerful, hearty feeling that everyone was his comrade.

'These Party members, young Baldur. Watch out for 'em, boy! Fine fellows, though, fine fellows.' And here Uncle Siegfried's double chins had wobbled and flushed out the spilled champagne from their creases. 'I make guns and tanks for them and they give me ribbons and crosses and whatnot. But don't ever tangle with a Party member, young Baldur. The brownshirts might be smashed up by the Fuhrer – and a damn good thing, too – although don't say I said that, for God's sake – but the Nazis run things, boy, run everything, and if you want to sleep safely in bed at nights, never cross 'em. Never.' He'd hiccoughed then, and belched, and knocked two glasses over from the broad table with its array of empty bottles. 'It ain't healthy, young Baldur, you take heed . . .'

There was no denying Party members got on. For an instant Wolz's fingers brushed the Nazi eagle and swastika badge on his right breast. His father had worn a crown above the three rings of a Korvettenkapitan. The son wore merely a star above his ring.

His attention was brought back by Gunther Blaum's handling of the fragile metal members of the kite. The metal rang as the skeleton fuselage was withdrawn from the cylinder.

'Take more care, you jumping jackass!' bellowed Wolz, once more a fiery-tempered, evil-intentioned, punishment-crazy and strict disciplinarian of the U-boat service. 'You idiot! If that strut is damaged you're on punishment!'

'Very good, sir,' said Gunther Blaum, an electrician and a man very knowledgeable about circuits and fuses.

Wolz bent over the metal kite.

The thing was perfectly designed to perform the job for which the U-boat carried it. A single strong tube braced by a pair of arched members supported the foot controls, the stick, the pilot's seat, the massive upright carrying the rotor, and the fin and rudder. No damage appeared to have been done.

The Focke-Achgelis FA-330 Bachstelze was a wonderful contraption, no doubt about that. The hands had it assembled now and were running out the towing cable. The air filled Wolz's nostrils with the warm humidity of the tropics. He glanced up. Up there the air would be fresher and the breeze would clear his head of unpleasant memories.

A leading hand fixed the parachute's two broad restraining bands against its seating on the upright. Wolz went methodically over every part of the water wagtail. It rested on its two skids, held down by the working party, and already the free-running rotors were revolving. The three blades circled gently, the controls holding down the pitch. Great care taken now paid dividends. The time to hurry would be when the kite was being winched in and packed away in the cylinders, perhaps when the U-boat was waiting desperately to dive.

'All set!'

He climbed into the seat and strapped in. Despite the heat he wore regulation flying togs. The stick felt warm in his grasp. His feet slid under the straps and pressed the controls experimentally. The rudder responded.

'Very good!'

Kapitanleutnant Ludecke looked over from the conning tower. The breeze of the boat's progress remained constant. The water sloshed past, spreading in creamy surges, pooled with deeper blues, running aft past the saddle tanks and the casing.

At Wolz's command the kite cast off and at once the rotors, driven by the wind, revolving into a blur of silver, lifted the Bachstelze off the deck. Always a tricky moment, this . . .

The kite slewed and Wolz brought her back on line directly aft of the boat. The cable paid out. He spoke into the microphone. 'Pay out . . . Pay out . . .'

Up he went, soaring above the U-boat, the vanes whirling, the air rushing past his head. There was no such thing as a windscreen. Anyway, by the very nature of the kite, he could only travel at the speed of the boat towing him, unless he did something foolish and veered off course, or dived.

Ahead and below U-42 plugged on across the sea, a long lean cigar-shape of grey steel, sleek and deadly. Her bow wave broke to either side and the creamy wash rolled away from her saddle tanks in a broad frothing trail that passed directly under Wolz. The Commander and the watch were looking up at him. He did not wave down. Ludecke was as likely as not to muster him for punishment for so lacking the qualities of an officer.

Up here, some hundred and thirty to hundred and fifty metres above the sea, visibility was extended by a considerable amount, from five miles or so from the boat's conning tower to something like twenty-five. He took a long careful look all about, using his Zeiss glasses on the second sweep, making sure the movements of his craft did not cause him to skip a single degree of arc in that searching sweep.

Nothing.

Well, they had been extraordinarily lucky with *Willowmore*. Her captain had been a resourceful fellow. He had taken a wide sweep out into the Atlantic and he'd tried to fight them off with his gun, quite in the way of the English trap ships of the last war. But nothing had availed him, in the end ...

As Wolz felt the breeze on him and revelled in the sensation of flying, he was forced to admit that there were things in Kapitanleutnant Ludecke's handling of their first sinking that struck him as not quite right. The torpedo had been fired just about as close as a torpedo might and have any hope of hitting. The pistol had functioned, and for that Baldur Wolz gave great thanks. He had worked on the pistols, again ...

Had the pistol malfunctioned and the fish failed to explode it was perfectly plain whose head would have been on the chopping-block.

'Nothing in sight, Baldur?'

Ludecke's voice rattled in over the headphones.

'Nothing. Nothing but sea and sky—'

'Keep your eyes peeled. The British have their damned Armed Merchant Cruisers at sea by now. I'd like one of those for lunch.'

'Very good, sir.'

Ludecke's flamboyant laugh crackled up the wire.

'You sound as though you're promising me one!'

'I'd like to, sir. But I think that Mr. Churchill might object, and that would never do.'

Ludecke laughed again. He was not one of your icy-cold, austere, punctilious Prussian officers. A warm-hearted man from the South, from Uberlingen on the Bodensee, a man who had learned his sailing on the lake and could remember the lean shapes of the Zeppelins floating in remote grandeur in the sky above.

'Mr. Churchill may have been taken back to the British Admiralty; as a notorious warmonger he will object to what the U-boats do. But we'll stick a bigger cigar than any he smokes right up him, yes, and laugh as we do it!'

Whilst concurring with these views, Baldur Wolz would have expressed them differently.

How marvellous it was to float through the sky, with the breeze on your face, the wind in your hair! Wolz had experienced no difficulties whatsoever in mastering the simple controls of the Bachstelze. He had taken up with great enthusiasm the sport of gliding which had swept Germany. To float free as a bird in the sky! Yes, he had been tempted, greatly tempted, and Uncle Siegfried had pressed with champagne eloquence, but in the end he had decided not to join the Luftwaffe. His cousin Manfred had joined up, sharing Wolz's enthusiasm for the air, and taking it to its logical conclusion. Manfred had piloted a Messerschmitt Bf 109 in the glorious victory of Poland, and wrote glowingly on his exploits. The 109, Manfred would say, cocking back his Luftwaffe cap and smiling, his bronzed and handsome face like that of a Nordic hero, was a far superior aircraft to the much-vaunted English Spitfire. So far, the two types had not clashed, for the war proceeded on a most curious course, and all activity seemed to lie with the Navy.

Wolz kept a sharp look-out for the state of the wind. The U-boat would only fly her kite off with a fresh enough breeze. It was more of an undignified scramble to recover the kite when the wind dropped than anything else, and Wolz did not altogether relish a ducking. For all he knew there was a shark out there whose predatory eye was fixed on the boat with every intention of snapping up anything which tumbled off. Whether the morsel fell from the boat or the sky, the shark wouldn't mind one whit.

Still nothing showed in that circle of sight save the sea and sky parted by the vague haze of the tropical horizon. The sun shone splendidly and the few clouds fluffed along like cargo ships ready for a tinfish.

The heat in the boat could be trying. Wolz relished the sensation of flying, even if the warm air seemed at times to flow past him like the waves from a steam bath. He swayed the kite from side to side, gently, feeling the rotors pulling, the strain on the cable, wishing that he could cast off and rise up and up and sport among those clouds. Mind you, he'd have to be equipped with a fish or two . . .

'Make a last check and then we'll haul you in, Baldur.'

The Commander's voice sounded imperturbable. Tomorrow or the next day would see them squarely astride the long lines of communication up from the Cape. 'Willi is champing to go.'

'Very good.'

Wolz conducted another long and searching sweep of the horizon. Nothing. Not the single hint of a smear of smoke, not a single masthead in sight. Somewhat depressed, Baldur was hauled back to the deck of U-42 and, after securing the kite, unstrapped and jumped down. He stretched.

Willi blazed with enthusiasm.

'Did you uncap your glasses, Baldur?'

'I'll uncap something more you won't fancy, young Willi.'

'Let someone who has eyes go aloft – then we'll see!'

But during his time aloft Willi Weidman had no more luck than Wolz.

Calling the rotor-kites water wagtails was a nice conceit. Wolz glanced aloft, up the gracefully curving thread of the cable. The Bachstelze looked like a monstrous dragonfly with silver wings hovering over the boat.

The next day brought a change in their fortunes.

Wolz was aloft. He could see, by all the indications that an honest sailorman would understand, that the wind was backing. As the pilot of the kite he felt the response as a flier would. The steady north-easterly was backing to the north, backing further and further around. Ludecke turned the head of his boat through the compass points, turning steadily to port; but he could not continue on an unprofitable course for too long.

'You'll have to descend, Baldur. Make it neat. I shall time you and the crew.'

Looking down Wolz fixed his glasses on the conning tower.

The Commander held his stop-watch in his hand. The glass face caught the sun and blinked back in a brilliant dot of fire.

'Very good, sir. One last look around.'

'Make it fast!'

Wolz went steadily around the horizon. He passed through west and north, went steadily along through north-east. Due east he went and then paused. His head turned back to the left. For a long instant he looked.

Was it? Could he be sure? Was that a thin smear of smoke, or was it some trick of the imagination?

'Come on, Baldur!'

'A moment, sir!'

'What is it?'

The sharpness of Ludecke's voice echoed Wolz's precise answer.

'A moment, sir.'

'I'll give you two minutes.'

Wolz wiped the glasses carefully, pressed them up against his eyes. Then he trained the glasses just off centre, aiming to place the mysterious object – smear of smoke, low-lying cloud, whatever – at the best point of vision. It was an old trick.

Yes. He felt sure. That smear of grey rose thin and firm until the top was blown away.

It had to be.

'Smoke, broad on the starboard beam.'

As soon as the words left his mouth Wolz felt the kite being pulled in as fast as the winch could haul.

The U-boat bustled with ordered activity. The kite came down. It hit the deck with a thump and Wolz waited until the hands had grasped it firmly and securely before he unbelted and jumped down.

'Move it, you lubbers! *Jump!*'

The kite was ripped into pieces and stuffed away in the cylinders in record time. Wolz drove the men, but there was no need. Everyone was caught up in the dramatic excitement of the moment. This was why they had been sent on this extended patrol. Donitz had risked two of his submarines, U-40 and U-42, on a long patrol to see what fat pickings might come their way before the English had a proper chance to put into full effect all their plans for the war at sea.

Was another *Willowmore* ploughing steadily on over the sea, waiting and ready to be sent to the bottom? Or was it an Armed Merchant Cruiser over there? Or a real cruiser? Perhaps she was a destroyer with racks full of depth-charges for U-42? Feeling the excitement in him, Wolz finished with the kite and dropped down the conning tower.

The diesels rumbled up to full power. U-42 was off after another kill.

CHAPTER FIVE

William Jones, Chief Engineer of S.S. *Bhatkal*, wiped the sweat away from his furrowed, dog-eaten face and thereby transferred a long black streak of oil to join all the other streaks and stains of his profession. He was usually called Dai, because he was a Welshman and there were three other Joneses aboard.

'Goddamn and blast this rustbucket!' he said, and stamped across the slats of the engine room to the speaking tube. He took a deep breath before he blew hard, hoping to blow some sense into the skipper. G. S. Hardisty, Master of *Bhatkal*, was a crusty old sea-devil, and he was demanding of his Chief Engineer miracles that were not to be had this side of a Newcastle refit.

'Bridge.'

'Now look here, skipper – If you want ten knots I can give you ten knots, and if you want the funnel as clean as a virgin's bottom I can do that for you – but, Godammit all to hell, I can't do both!'

'You can make ten knots without smoke, Chief—'

'Maybe I could when this ship was new-built in time for the Crimean War! Ease her down, and I'll guarantee no smoke, or not much. But you'll have smoke at ten knots.'

The sound of the sigh at the other end of the voice-pipe further infuriated Dai Jones. It wasn't his fault.

'We've had news there's a Jerry raider in the area.'

'Well ease down, man! He'll as like do fifteen knots. Go down to revolutions for seven and a half – maybe eight – and, look, you, you'll have no smoke at all.'

No doubt the skipper was digesting that. It made the sweetest of sweet sense to Jones. But then, he only ran the engines and oiled them and cajoled them and talked to them. Those windswept high-and-mighty deck officers decided what his engines would do. Or at least they thought they did.

'I'd like to clear the area as fast as possible, Chief.'

The snort Dai Jones let fly made the skipper wince.

'Well – you'll have smoke, man!'

'I'll accept that for another two hours. After that—'

The voicepipe emitted a distant sound like a cough followed by a gabble. And then, so loud it made Dai Jones step back, a rush of profanity that bounced around the ancient engine room.

When the skipper stopped swearing he bellowed down the pipe: 'Chief! We've just sighted a submarine. Yes, a bloody sub! I want everything you've got! I don't give a damn how much smoke you make!'

'You'll get all these poor engines can give, and after that we'll all go to perdition together!'

Jones slammed the whistle back and roared into his black gang. *Bhatkal* had a single screw powered by an old reciprocating engine that Isambard Kingdom Brunel would have looked at askance, and a boiler with plating so thin chewing gum might patch it admirably. Now Jones set his stokers into furious action, opening the steam pipes to full, keeping his eyes on the gauges and cursing and putting on more steam when the engines trembled over into the red.

Goddamn Jerry U-boat! What the hell was the thing doing out here in the middle of nowhere? And what about that tomfool raider the skipper had spoken of? Was this just another of the usual foul-ups of those chairborne idiots at the Admiralty?

S.S. *Bhatkal*, all four thousand tons of her, chugged along belching smoke, with sparks flying from her tall skinny funnel, desperately trying to outrun a modern U-boat.

No one, in either vessel, really thought it was funny.

'She'll blow herself up and save us the job,' observed Kapitanleutnant Ludecke. He laughed.

U-42 had eased down to twelve knots and now turned in to approach the steamer from the port bow. The sun shone over the starboard quarter and played in the flung spray from the bows. The old steamer – for she was old, anyone could see that – lurched along, belching smoke and flames. Ludecke felt quite affectionately disposed towards her. But he had to harden his heart. Despite her age she was carrying cargo to England, and carrying cargoes to England was an activity that Admiral Donitz had expressly forbidden.

'Put a round across her, Baldur,' he said. 'And then hit the radio shack. Although, judging from the rest of her, I doubt her wireless will work, it'll be so old and moth-eaten.'

'Very good!'

Wolz directed the gunner as ordered and the shots cracked out, flat and spiteful. It would be dark soon, with the sun sliding down towards the horizon, and this job must be finished before the Englander sought escape in the darkness.

A puff of smoke shot up from the bridge.

'Make sure' bellowed Ludecke. 'Shoot until she stops.'

The 3.7 centimetre rounds might not carry the crushing punch of the 10.5 centimetre, but they smashed into the thin plates and the light scantlings of *Bhatkal*, and very soon the volume of black smoke lessened, the sparks stopped shooting high from the lean funnel, and the white froth under the counter fell away. S.S. *Bhatkal* surged ever more slowly through the water until she came to a queasy halt, gently rocking with the motion of the sea.

All the U-boat men topsides could see she had no defensive armament mounted.

Kapitanleutnant Ludecke was taking no chances.

'If she is a U-boat trap ship ...'

He knew the drill worked out. He'd have no mercy whatsoever on a Q-ship. He wondered just how long it would take the English to equip a ship to spring the trap. An old rustbucket like this sailing from a foreign port? No – hardly likely. But he would take no chances.

'No sign of anyone left on deck, sir,' reported the look-out.

Ludecke made no comment. Wait.

The two boats pulled away most untidily, the oars rising and falling and water splashing. They had no great distance to go to reach the African coast. To take prisoners was out of the question. The Master and the Chief Engineer ought to be questioned, but that must wait until he was sure this pathetic old steamer was all she seemed to be and no more.

Down below Meisten had found a silhouette in the book that he thought could well be this floating junk-yard. The very fact that such an insignificant vessel had been included in the U-boat handbook of enemy shipping indicated the thoroughness of the German Navy department and the U-boat Service. *Willowmore* had been positively identified by her name; this float-ing scrapheap's name was mostly obscured by streaks of rust and flaked paint. 'kal' was all that was visible.

'*Bhatkal*, sir,' said Meisten and Ludecke acknow-ledged briefly. No signal had been got off; the ship's wireless had not operated either because there had been no time or, as Ludecke had suggested, because it was in the same condition as the rest of the vessel.

'Four thousand tons.'

'That'll make thirteen thousand four hundred,' said Ludecke. 'It's a start.'

Tonnages sunk obsessed all U-boat men.

Ludecke was not prepared to waste a torpedo on this ancient derelict.

'Baldur – use your shooting eye. Make some confetti along her waterline.'

'Very good.'

45

Wolz had no doubt the 3.7 could do this job. The plates of this rustbucket couldn't be much thicker than tissue paper and the 3.7 should do the job without trouble.

The gunner opened up on command and soon the shells were blatting out. The sun slid down the sky. The wind was backing even further and a gale might easily be sweeping in across the broad wastes of the Atlantic. But this job must be done first. Wolz saw the hits. He saw the leap and spout of white water. The crash of the gun and the acrid bite of burnt cordite blended in his mind, so that he could almost imagine this to be some important action instead of – and then, as Ludecke bellowed: 'Cease fire!' he realised that, by God, this was important.

This was what the maritime war against England was all about. There were thousands of ships like this ploughing the seas and bringing their invaluable cargoes through to England. To stop even one of them was to score a victory. Even so old and moth-eaten a ship as this *Bhatkal* represented value to England afloat and value to Germany sunk.

'She's going!' yelled the look-out on watch.

Everyone could see that.

Steam gushed up. The hull sank lower. She went down by the head and with a lurching roll to port where Wolz's shells had punched confetti holes in her pathetically thin side.

A great boiling cauldron of foam and steam burst up. The boiler blew as she slid below and a mushroom of debris-laden water fountained up. It hissed as it plunged back to the sea.

'Steer for the boats,' said Ludecke crisply, breaking the spell of the moment.

Wolz remained closed up at the gun whilst Meisten went forward along the deck. The First Officer looked lean and elegant against the last of the light. Ludecke leaned over the coaming of the conning tower.

'You can bring the master and the chief engineer aboard, Number One. No-one else.'

'Very good.'

The boats fended off from the U-boat's steel casing. They bobbed gently. The gale brooming down would not reach them yet. Men stared up, white faces tinted now by the last of the rapid sunset. The whole scene looked weird and unreal to Ludecke. But he had his duty to do.

'Go for'ard, Number Two. Use your English on 'em.'

Wolz gave a clipped order to the gunners at the 3.7 and then ran along the boat.

A wave caught his ankle, but he disregarded it and sped on. A figure was waving its arms from the boat and a darker mass showed at the end of a line. The hands with Meisten were hauling a man aboard. Wolz heard the shouts.

'Let me get at the bloody black bastard! He's killed the skipper! Poor old Hardisty! Blown right out of his boots, so he was! I'll bash the sod's head in!'

'Chief!' a voice yelled frantically from the lifeboat. 'Dai! They've got guns! Come back here, you stupid Welsh bastard!'

'I'll give the boyos guns!'

Wolz, going forward, saw the dark mass at the end of the line straighten up. A small, spare, energetic man scrambled up. The sun caught a glint from the six-inch spanner he carried, lifted high. That spanner would crunch down on the head of the nearest German sailor . . .

Wolz saw it all.

The sailor, one of the foredeck party, dodged back, shouting a Bremerhaven oath. The little man, who must be the Chief Engineer of the sunk *Bhatkal*, let rip some strange expression that was not English or German, and charged for Meisten. The big spanner looked ugly in the fast-dying day.

Calmly, Meisten flicked open his holster. He took out the Luger. He levelled it. The automatic spat fire.

Three times it fired.

The Chief reared upright, clawing. The spanner dropped from his fingers. The clang as it hit the casing echoed weirdly over that golden-lit scene.

Then the little man fell. He pitched forward, and rolled sideways, and slipping and slopping and trailing a line of spilled blood, like a crushed insect, he toppled over the side.

CHAPTER SIX

Hans Rudermann gave a last proprietary rub over the labouring diesel with his oily rag and stepped back. He moved like a cat in the cramped confines of the engine room. The noise of the diesels, the inevitable fumes, the occasional vicious spurt of flame, were all alike to him – mere parts of his trade. He looked across at Klaus Hencke and the two men moved to the quietest part of the compartment to resume their argument.

'All the same, Hans, there was nothing else Number One could have done. That mad Englishman was trying to brain me!'

'You jumped away quickly enough.'

'Damn right! So would you have done.'

'But to shoot him down, like that—'

'Don't tell me you're going soft on the blasted English!'

'If we weren't on duty I'd twist your neck for that, Klaus!'

With the pungent, peculiar, never-forgotten stink of a U-boat all about them, the two wrangled on. U-42 lunged on over a mounting sea, the spray breaking from her bows and whipping back bitingly over the conning tower, drenching the watch, making life uncomfortable. Because he had to, the Commander had turned her head into the wind. He would ride out what he might of the gale on the surface. Like any U-boat man he treasured his batteries.

The watches changed and Ruderman and Hencke could sprawl out in their hammocks and, leaning over, try to play a hand or two of Skat. The subject of Oberleutnant Meisten's rapid action in shooting the mad Englishman occupied them all. Most approved whole-heartedly. The idiot had raved in like a maniac waving an enormous spanner and deserved to be shot. The others, and there were few of them, contented themselves with pointing out that the Chief Engineer of *Bhatkal* had been a civilian. But, as the Coxswain, Rudi Goehle, a bluff and competent man from Kiel, said to crush what he considered an ill-advised argument: 'Civilian or not, he tried to bash the Oberleutnant's skull in. This is a war in which everyone is involved.' He'd given his wide, apparently genial smile that hid a driving power of conviction, bolstered by his total belief in the destiny of Germany. 'If the fool didn't want to be killed he should never have shipped out – he's gone the way all the damned English will go.'

Willi Weidman, on duty in the control room at the time, had not witnessed the incident.

'You can't blame Meisten, Baldur. I think I'd have done the same thing.'

'Probably, Willi.' Wolz found, to his dismay, that he couldn't quite sort out his own feelings. The sight of that pathetic little figure, spilling blood, slipping over the side of the U-boat affected him. His English friends had studiously avoided the subject of the last war during his visits. But he'd overheard enough, in wardrooms, in pubs down by the dockyards, to tell him the English were prickly on the subject of submarine warfare. It was to them unsporting. Wolz had read his Kipling, along with Mein Kampf, and knew of flannelled fools and muddied oafs, But the English put so much of their sport into their ideas of warfare they must be hopelessly muddled in their appreciation of what war was all about.

So he said: 'The man's dead and his ship is sunk. It's just more tonnage to hoist when we return.'

'We'll have a full rig of pennants, you'll see!' declared Willi, with enthusiastic conviction.

Kapitanleutnant Gustav Ludecke also shared that

conviction. But with the Chief he stared again at the figures. Fuel oil was being used, and these high-speed dashes consumed the precious stuff at an enormous rate. As the U-boat plunged up and down in the sea, with Meisten in the conning tower drenched from head to toe, the Chief and Ludecke calculated the consumption forecasts and the distances to be covered.

In sending out two boats so far this early in the war Donitz was making a declaration, nailing his colours to the mast. The type IIs and the type VIIs could operate around Britain and to a respectable distance into the Atlantic. But to interfere with British sea-borne commerce wider afield the ocean-going type IXs were vital. The fiasco of being ordered to support the doomed *Graf Spee* had devoured a deal more of their fuel than was comfortable. So Ludecke had to keep restraining himself from poking his head into the wireless cubby and chivvying the operator.

The regular signals from BdU informed him a raider was in the area, and once contact was made and a rendezvous organised he would be able to top up his tanks. He'd also take on more torpedoes and pray the pistols would work. But, until then, he must rigidly conserve every ounce of fuel.

Donning his oilskins and picking up the big sou'-wester he climbed up the ladder and poked his head out of the hatch. Wind and spray slashed him. He climbed out and saw the three men on watch as dark, water-running figures, hunched shapes against the steel plating, dark and barely made out.

'All correct, Gunther?'

'All correct. She's corkscrewing—' Meisten broke off as U-42 stuck her nose down and broke a solid wall of water over her coaming. The feel of it told the men on the conning tower – the water smashed into them from the darkness with a stunning force, drenching them, spraying everywhere. Almost instantly as the boat's head dropped over the roller another spurting mass of foam-laced water battered them.

Ludecke got his breath back and wiped his streaming eyes.

'Right. Secure for diving, Number One.'

'Very good.'

Ludecke waited for the others to go down. He could see nothing in the gale-lashed darkness. Some skippers would hold on in a blow like this, exulting in their seamanship. As he had told Wolz in an early blow on their way across the Bay: 'The advantage of a U-boat is that she can dive under the weather. Never be too proud to take advantage of that, Baldur – provided, of course, your batteries are in good shape.'

Out here in the middle of nowhere he could run all day on the surface recharging batteries. Out here there were no inquisitive and noisy-depth-charge-throwing English destroyers to annoy an honest U-boat man. He dropped down the hatch feeling pleased that he was, in truth, a U-boat man and not some poor surface fellow who had nowhere to go in a gale of wind.

The hatch cover slammed and drops of water splattered his face. He sealed up, dropped down through the hatch in the pressure hull and span the wheel, clipping up. Looking around the comfortable white-painted interior of his boat, brightly lit, he felt at home. The gauges winked back at him like old friends. The duty watch cared for their instruments. The bubble was kept beautifully on line as the boat rode evenly, and yet forty metres above their heads the surface of the sea was churned into mountains of water as tons and tons of the stuff flung itself about in phenomenal abandon. Down here all was calm.

He carried out a careful check just to make sure everything was all right. Pride and all that ... But Meisten and Wolz and Weidman knew their jobs, and the Chief could make a diesel or an electric motor run like a sewing-machine.

So, going to his cabin, Kapitanleutnant Gustav Ludecke considered himself the most fortunate of men.

When Baldur Wolz came off watch he stretched out on his bunk and closed his eyes. But he did not sleep. He did not keep a diary, and his mind remained actively running over recent events. Perhaps there was a touch of unadmitted fatalism in that decision, taken quietly and consciously, not to keep a diary. Perhaps the dark shadow of the father he had never known, of the thousands of U-boat men who had sunk in the first war, motivated him.

But this time, with the new U-boats and with Rear-Admiral Donitz at the helm, and with the decadence of the English, this time it would be different!

The boat existed about him. The smell of pitch and oil and sea water existed, it was real, it was life. The distant thrilling of the motors did not disturb him; that was real, too, and a part of life. The long gentle movements of the boat under him lulled him, but he did not sleep. That Lottie! He thought about her quite as much as he did about Lisl – but in a way at once more scarlet and erotic and lurid. Lisl remained pure and undefiled, and however much he might scoff at his own priggish and jejune feelings about his cousin, that did not stop him from feeling them. The idea that she might relish a tumble just as much as Lottie could only penetrate his brain in a sidelong, instantly banished way, shamefaced, as though he dirtied himself.

Lisl remained Lisl, and if, by supreme good fortune, he could marry her one day – he would, by God!

Lottie's friend Heidi had proved co-operative on the following day, the day after the party, and the three of them had had a fine old time. Still and all, Heidi didn't *romp* as well as Lottie . . .

That made him think of Marlene, his cousin Siegfried's uninhibited friend. He had never discovered her surname. Cousin Siegfried was the eldest son and thus named for his father. He had early taken whole-heartedly to the National Socialist Party and the S.S. had taken him in and moulded him until, although still Cousin Siegfried, he had become a different person from that old Cousin Siegfried with whom Baldur Wolz and the others had tussled and played pranks and got up to all kinds of mischief in the schloss and its surrounding acres.

Marlene was slender and tall with long blonde hair and pale blue eyes, and a straight nose like the cutwater of a destroyer. Her mouth might be a little on the thin side for someone with truly voluptuous tastes, to be sure.

Siegfried had thrown a party for his friends. They were not the same crowd of helter-skelter life-loving villains with whom Manfred of the Luftwaffe and Baldur of the Navy mixed. There were mostly young S.S. officers, a few serving officials of the Party, civil servants, a local landowner's sons. They represented a new and powerful force in the life of the Fatherland, and Uncle Siegfried had wisely taken himself off for a visit to Berlin whilst his eldest son entertained.

A great deal of beer was drunk, in the old German way, but schnapps and champagne flowed as freely. The uniforms glittered. Black – yes, that was the colour, black tunics and jackets, black breeches, black boots, and the red and white of the swastikas. Silver braid was everywhere.

As a Naval officer, Wolz had donned a civilian suit and joined the other guests and the party had roared along in familiar style through the small hours.

The huge hall of the schloss blazed with heat and light, with many candles burning down now but still tall, adding their lustre to the electrically-lit chandeliers. Enormous log fires burned on the four hearths. Stag and boar heads and other trophies of the hunt glimmered from the walls. The S.S. officers grew tired of dancing with the girls to the gramophone and soon began to bellow out old German songs – and the new songs of a revitalised Fatherland.

Wolz, sitting comfortably in a leather armchair near the largest of the fires, a magnum wedged down between him and the arm of the chair, did not join in but was content to listen and watch the firelight reflected on the flushed faces of the singers. Siegfried it was who started the chant.

'Marlene! Marlene!'

Curtains had been rigged between the fires across one end of the hall. The half-drunken men gathered, perched on seats, sitting on the floor, swaying with their arms about one another's shoulders, spilling wine. 'Marlene!'

Wolz looked at the curtains. They parted in the centre and a dramatic figure all swathed in a black cloak appeared.

The bedlam grew into a frightful racket.

The girl's long blonde hair shook free, her face held down against her arms folding the cloak upwards. It was dramatic – no doubt of that.

Abruptly she straightened. Her face, dead white, brilliant, appeared fixed in a trance. Her reddened lips split into a wide smile, a beckoning, inviting, lascivious smile. Apart from that wide-smiling painted mouth no other expression marred the faultlessness of her pale face.

Abruptly, as the record someone had placed on the turntable reached a blaring crescendo of trumpets, she threw her arms wide.

Wolz – for all he was a tough U-boat man – gasped.

Marlene stood forth, shining, superb, blasphemous.

She wore brilliantly polished black boots. She wore a regulation S.S. belt and straps and a holstered Walther automatic. She wore an S.S. cap at a jaunty angle, clapped on her head as she swirled the cloak aside. The effect was stunning. Her body gleamed in the lights. The ruby firelight played against her thighs, rounding them with ruddy light and purple shadows. Her breasts trembled as she moved, painted, proud, and the final riveting touch showed itself between those perfect breasts. Swinging from a thin golden chain a swastika bounced between her breasts, touching first one and then the other, maddeningly.

As she went through her act and sang her songs, for she was an actress from Berlin, Wolz admitted to himself that he was confused. She was a delicious piece, undoubtedly. But she was also blatantly flaunting her sexuality in almost blasphemous circumstances. The S.S. trappings about her nakedness served merely to emphasize that nakedness – no! No, not merely. The two meshed. But – the S.S. officers along with all the rest were roaring their approval, joining in the choruses, shouting lewd remarks, smoking cigarettes and stubbing them out and lighting more with feverish movements. Their eyes devoured the nude form of Marlene. But, to Wolz, their actions were almost incomprehensible.

Oh, yes – his Navy comrades would have roared out their appreciation. Manfred's Luftwaffe pilots would have rushed in with propellers flying. But – the S.S.? How did this square with the philosophy of the Fuhrer? What would Himmler say if he could see the pride of his officers now?

The rest of the evening had passed in a different and yet wholly familiar way as Wolz had been waylaid and entrapped and finally captured by a dark-haired girl from Berlin whose escort was snoring dead drunk under the stairs with two other bodies deposited upon him – Uncle Siegfried had not had the taste to install the best Nazi-designed vomitorium – and who would know nothing, she swore, until much later on the next day.

So, Wolz had enjoyed himself, picking up what crumbs of life he could when he could. But, all the same, he had not cared to remark on his puzzlement to

Cousin Siegfried after the last of the guests had left.

All Siegfried said in his heavy way, was: 'A good party, yes, Baldur? You enjoyed yourself?'

'Yes, Siegfried. Very much.' And then he had ventured: 'I am glad to see the S.S. can let their hair down as much as the Navy.'

Siegfried turned his sharp-jawed, heavy face towards Wolz. 'Cousin,' said Siegfried. 'Whatever you hear about the S.S. – believe it.'

There was nothing a Navy man could say to that.

Siegfried finished the conversation by a reference to their plans for the following day – a visit to a neighbour whose husband had recently died and in whose daughter Siegfried had an interest – and by saying: 'At least, my dear Baldur, we are not like the S.A., a bunch of perverts.'

'No,' said Baldur Wolz. 'No, indeed.'

His thoughts twined fitfully around that visit the next day to the Baroness von Hartstein and her daughter Trudi and the scheme which had infiltrated his evil brain; but U-42 continued to glide smoothly beneath the tempestuous waters of the Atlantic and he was healthily tired and his eyelids closed and he slept. His last thought, oddly enough, was not of the greasy trail of blood from that idiot of an English engineer sliding over the casing; rather it was of the swastika, glittering in the lights, bumping to and fro between Marlene's trembling breasts.

Like any sensible man, the Captain of the Armed Merchant Cruiser *Saltburn Head* liked his kai scalding hot, so Captain's Steward Alf Perkins ran. The enamel mug balanced against the wild heavings of the ship, he bucketed his way onto the bridge. *Saltburn Head* had been a passenger liner, built stoutly at Harland and Wolff's in Belfast back in '24, and her bridge lofted so high it was a fair old scarper up the ladders.

'Right, Alf, thanks.'

Captain Clarence Manning wrapped his thick hands around the mug and sniffed the fragrance. About him the men on watch were looking forward to their kai, and the big ship ran well through the tumultuous sea. A few dim lights scattered vague reflections across the darkened bridge. The binnacle light gleamed occasionally as Captain Manning turned to make a scarcely-needed check. The sense of this large old vessel all about him ought to have reassured him; but even Captain's Steward Perkins could see the skipper was not a really happy man.

Perkins ducked back off the bridge to reach his own cubby. He'd run off from the row of tenements in Bermondsey when he'd been a nipper in the hopes of finding employment, cash and adventure at sea. Stewarding around the Cape for a space had made him think the sea would be his life, and then Grace had looked at him, and he'd felt the old urge in a very different and surprising form, so they'd got married and he'd found a job in a caff and thought he'd settled down in Stockwell.

And then bloody Adolf had come along and mucked everything up. So Alf Perkins had gone back to sea in the only trade he knew, stewarding. Mind you, this was supposed to be a cruiser of the Royal Navy, although the engine room staff had run her in peacetime. He had been shown a Lewis gun and told how to pop a drum off and how to clear a stoppage. He reasoned out for himself that you pulled the trigger to fire the machine-gun. As for aiming – the old Leading Seaman who'd bashed a few thoughts about Lewis guns into his head had said: 'Just point it and squirt. You just hope the bugger'll get scared and fly away.'

So *Saltburn Head*, with her eight six-inch guns – none of which had been manufactured later than a few years before the opening of World War One – had trundled off to war escorting convoys. Now she was assisting in the search for this damned Jerry raider in the Atlantic – and Steward Perkins did not like what he saw in the Captain's face.

He had to keep the Lewis gun on the starboard bridge wing cleaned, bright, and slightly oiled, and he did this with the same quick, deft, finicky movements he washed and dried cups and saucers in the caff at home, or served the skipper's dinner as the old *Saltburn Head* rolled along.

As for any hope of finding another ship at sea on a night like this, that was quite out of the question unless they rammed her. *Saltburn Head* was sixteen thousand three hundred and twenty tons gross, five hundred and forty-two feet three inches between perpendiculars, and her two-shaft reciprocating engines were supposed to put out no less than 15,000 I.H.P. The Chief swore blind if they did they'd blow the funnel sky-high; all the same, he had got her up to sixteen knots, although blacking out half the sky, that time of the scare on a run up from Gib.

At their stations about the ship as she lunged on through the sea the men of *Saltburn Head* expressed blind confidence in their skipper, who had promised them to go in baldheaded if there was the slightest hint of action. She might still look something like a passenger liner with her tall funnel and towering superstructure, although the fancy cabins had been cleared away to form messdecks, and her rust streaks and down-at-heels appearance; yet the men polished up their guns, and hoped. They had a couple of three-inch ack-ack. God knew where they'd come from. Salvaged from a wreck, probably.

And so, as the Armed Merchant Cruiser bucketed through the gale, every now and then one of her company of two hundred and fifty souls would think of *Rawalpindi*, and grow quiet.

Instead of *Rawalpindi* up there in the vicious beastliness of a North Atlantic winter it could have been *Saltburn Head*. She might have been crushed and destroyed under the rain of eleven-inch shells from *Scharnhorst* and *Gneisenau*. Each man knew that had *Saltburn Head* been there, Captain Manning would have taken her in, her fragile plates and her ridiculous antiquated armament notwithstanding. That was what being in the Royal Navy was all about.

Captain's Steward Alf Perkins pottered in his cubby, and contemplated his future with a promise that once he got back to the caff in Stockwell after the war he'd blooming well never even sail on one of the Eagles down the Thames to Southend.

Not likely.

The S.S. *Algahoinas*, or the S.S. *Nakaminato*, or the S.S. *Makeyevka*, or – the name under which she had been commissioned and sailed from Bremerhaven – the S.S. *Rugen*, plunged her eight thousand three hundred tons from one wave crest to the next, ploughing doggedly out of the skirts of the gale. Many of her fake plywood ventilators had been ripped away. The for'ard starboard lifeboat had been stoved in. The ply and canvas deckhouse around the for'ard 15 centimetre gun had been shredded and only devoted efforts had hauled the confused, wind-flogged mess, spray-sodden, to safety.

Now Captain Klaus Frohlich, a determined Naval officer with an Armed Merchant Raider and three hundred and forty men under his command, stood with legs wide-braced on the bridge and debated whether to change his ship back to *Nakaminato Maru*, as soon as the gale abated, or adopt another of the disguises *Rugen* had up her sleeve.

The English knew he had operated off the west coast of Africa, and therefore it was high time he took himself off to other waters. Since the *Graf Spee* incident South America would not be healthy. Around the Cape lay all the splendid pickings of the Indian Ocean. Yes, Frohlich decided, yes, he would refuel this confounded U-boat, on orders, and then they could resume the task for which they had been despatched, the wholesale sinking of British merchantmen.

The forenoon watch had changed and the sea was visibly moderating. Now the spray-slashed deck of *Rugen* showed up the scars of the battle with the sea. Time enough to clear up when the next disguise was decided on. The sea still ran, greenly grey, driving on with enormous power from the wastes of the Atlantic. The sky remained overcast, but a watery sun peeped through every now and then. Soon they might expect a glimpse of the horizon.

At that moment the look-out bellowed.

'Ship in sight! Dead ahead—'

Frohlich jumped out onto the bridge wing and whipped his glasses to his eyes. In this weather the range of vision from the crow's nest and that from the bridge would be almost the same ... Yes. There she was, a damned great tanker lumbering along, waddling, spurting white water from her stern. He could even make out the muddy red splodge that was the British Red Ensign.

She was on the same course, driven as had been *Rugen* by the superior force of the gale. Frohlich let a small smile light his pale eyes. He lowered the glasses. A tanker, a beautiful fat tanker, delivered to him by the gods of the sea! Just what he needed to top up his bunkers in preparation for the run around the Cape, not to mention the U-boat who wished to guzzle from him, like a piglet sucking sustenance from her mother.

'Action stations! Get the civilian party on deck!'

Rugen bustled with activity. There would be a little wait until they drew up with the tanker. When they did they would appear just a simple storm-beaten tramp, inoffensive, rating a lordly signal from the tanker, a brief greeting as ships passed across the sea.

Then, and here Frohlich's smile widened, then the 15 centimetre guns would abruptly appear from their hidden mountings and the damned English tanker would understand she had been caught by a raiding tiger of the seas.

That, to Frohlich, was a moment to treasure.

He spoke to Oberleutnant zur See Anton, the Gunnery Officer.

'Knock the radio out with the first shot. But remember, she's a tanker. We need that fuel, so make sure you don't set her afire.'

'Very good, Herr Kapitan!'

So, contentedly, Frohlich brought *Rugen* steadily up on the English tanker, very pleased with the prospects for his immediate future.

CHAPTER SEVEN

Usually, Leutnant zur See Baldur Wolz when he emerged through the conning tower after the boat had been submerged would light one of those fierce black cheroots that champed up from the corner of his mouth. Usually; not always. Wolz deliberately attempted never to establish any routine pattern of life, apart from the necessary discipline of the U-boat service. He liked to keep his options open. If he did not light a cheroot on morning watch, then he fancied he had gained a little point of advantage in the eternal tussle against the rigours of ordered existence.

This morning, as he took over the watch, he extracted a black cheroot from the slim silver case in his breast pocket. He lit it with the expert cupping of hands any sailorman must cultivate. He drew in the smoke, thick and fragrant, and blew it out in streamers that were instantly whipped away by the breeze.

The signalman, glancing over, saw Wolz with his peaked cap at a jaunty angle, his chin stuck out, the black cigar thrusting up aggressively from the corner of his mouth, and he nudged the look-out.

'Look at him, Hans! He looks just like a pirate.'

'And like a pirate he'll sink a lot of tonnage.'

'Strict, though—'

Wolz half-turned. He could not hear the watch clearly, but they were jabbering away.

Mildly, he said: 'If you want to be on punishment by all means continue talking.'

Their mouths shut like sharks' jaws, click.

The sea had gone down, the sun was trying to poke a few thin streamers of light through the overcast, the breeze caught up only an occasional smash of spindrift. Yes, life was good, and, if all went well, on this day they'd pick up their fuel ration and torpedoes and a new breech for the gun, and be in fine fettle to continue the patrol.

As his watch wore on the weather improved with that amazing transformation he always found impressive. The night before the waves had rolled mountainous seas to smash and rend all in their path. Now, with the sun reaching the zenith, even the long rollers, aftermath of the gale, swirled with diminishing violence to say quite clearly that all was once more right with the world.

The horizon appeared again, picking up definition and clarity. The colour of the sea changed, melting away from those ominous dark greens to a smoother lighter blue. U-42 bore on over an enchanted sea.

Kapitanleutnant Ludecke hoisted himself up and stared all about the horizon. Wolz knew very well what the Skipper's next order would be.

'Willi can take the kite up. We can reach the rendezvous, take on our fuel, and be off before dark.'

So the Bachstelze was drawn from its cylinders and erected. Willi togged up, beaming, entranced at the prospect of floating above the boat and, as he said, being able to spit down on them if he felt like it. At this time Ludecke gave his men a chance to dry their clothes and air themselves on the casing. The chances of any enemy spotting them here in the wastes of ocean were so remote he felt not one whit that he was risking his command.

'Old Daddy'll look out for us,' said the hands, with complete confidence.

The men stripped off. Their bodies were bronzed enough, for duty in these hot climes gave splendid opportunities for sunbathing. Ludecke would not allow swimming or even surf-board riding. They might have to dive rapidly. They might. It was just possible some interfering English patrol might happen their way. If one did the men on deck could get below in a mad scramble with enough speed. With men skylarking in the water the chances would be seriously reduced.

Weidman floated aloft under his whirling rotors. Wolz looked up, chewing on the butt of his cigar. Hell! He'd looked forward to a flight today, and damned the tricky business of controlling the water wagtail. Willi was quite good at it, but he used about fifty per cent more effort than Wolz, and thus his look-out was that much reduced in effectiveness.

Up span the rotors, hauling the kite up and away from U-42. A giant dragonfly, hauled along against the wind, the Bachstelze fascinated anyone with imagination. Donitz, who had been promoted from Kommodore to Rear-Admiral in October, had been precise in his instructions. The British, he had said, had no idea that such a device as the gyro-kite existed and it was the duty of the U-boatmen to make sure they never discovered until far too late.

The idea of fooling the English appealed to Baldur Wolz. He chewed on his cigar and made sure the boat ran smoothly and contemplated some of the mad escapades he had got himself into during his visits to his English friends. They'd been a mad crowd. My God! That time they'd broken into the Captain's quarters and stolen his wife's underclothes and run them up the flagstaff! The furore! A pair of ample knickers and a pair of equally ample brassieres, floating in a force five! The scarlet of the faces! The roaring of voices – and the subs all killing themselves laughing with faces as long as those damned English horses he'd ridden so uncomfortably over fences and through ditches.

He was forced to contrast those diabolical nights with not only his English friends but also his comrades of the Navy, and stand them against what he sensed of the joys of fun and frolic in Cousin Siegfried's S.S. Marlene, naked, booted, strapped – the depth of the emotions in the S.S. men devouring her with their eyes

65

impressed Wolz, with a little shiver, as somehow cold, calculating, not the impetuous tallyho of the U-boat man, not that at all.

Willi swung the kite about, almost skylarking, although a too great abandonment to the joys of flying would bring a brusque reprimand barking up the telephone line.

Wolz knew little about the secret raiders that Admiral Raeder had authorised for this new war. He had read much of those great and epic voyages of the last war. Ships disguised to look like anything but themselves, they would lure an unsuspecting merchantman and then – boom. The story was the same – or almost the same – as when a U-boat broke surface and fired her gun. Still and all, Wolz felt keenly that with the naval preponderance possessed by Britain and France, the future success of the war at sea must lie with the submarine fleet. The Fuhrer had imposed strict limitations on what they might do. Goebbels had said the English themselves had sunk *Athenia*. Well, that was possible, just, in a world obsessed by propaganda values.

Not for the first time Wolz gave thanks that Raeder had kept the Navy out of politics. Why, the Grand Admiral had even managed to retain the chaplain's branch. The Nazi system had not touched the Navy, although every now and again an ardent Party member shipped out – as witness Meisten in U-42.

Wolz bore in mind his Uncle's strictures on the Party and on Party members, and steered well clear of them when he could. Willi, for instance, had been sucked into the Hitler Youth early, and even he, almost witless though he was, had confided to Wolz that he much preferred the atmosphere of the Navy.

Willi Weidman had been put through it well and truly when he'd gone through the preliminary training on Danholm. That was where the potential naval officer learned what it was like in the Army. Yes, Wolz could well imagine Willi, perpetually surprised, chasing up and down the hills wearing his respirator, cursing his ammunition boots, sweating, catching punishment duties as a matter of course. Had Willi been with Wolz the period would have been much lightened.

The sea was now greatly reduced. The boat's wake cut a broad swathe of cream tumbled foam through the glimmering blue. Nothing was in sight. The sun beat down and the men put on the wild assortment of hats they had made for these sunbathing sessions. Down below in the pressure hull the on-duty watch studied their gauges and checked their responsibilities and hoped their turn would come on deck before anything else happened to foul things up in the Navy way.

Kapitanleutnant Ludecke had stamped on the German sailor's natural predeliction for getting into fights. Scraps on shore, he'd say, are all right every now and then. Gets the old blood flowing, keeps the muscles toned up, gives the medics the chance of some practice and often does the dentists out of a job. But at sea — no. He meant what he said. A few days out Muller and Reuss, one from the engine room, the other a torpedoman, had started one of those friendly fights in which the rules are all implicit. They'd kicked and bashed and hit one another's heads against various hard edges, and tried to remove as many teeth as mutually possible.

There had been quite a row. Muller's right hand got caught somehow in Reuss's mouth and was snatched away with a tooth embedded. Reuss's lower anatomy had somehow got in the way of Muller's knee. Then the cheerful combatants, swearing away at each other, had been hauled apart. It was the considered opinion of the boat that Reuss, who was a lumbering fellow from Bavaria, had come off worse and Muller, a sharp number from Berlin, hadn't really deserved to win so handsomely.

As a fight it was a mere nothing compared to some of the scraps they'd all enjoyed ashore. But Ludecke had come down with all the weight of his authority and personality.

Clowns, he'd called them. Cretins, unmitigated morons. Reuss wasn't too sure what he meant, but Dieter had nudged him and whispered in his ear loud enough for all to hear: 'Daddy says you're a bloody idiot for fighting at sea.'

That made everyone feel better.

So the hands could sunbathe on the casing and carry on their duties below and Wolz felt pretty confident that they wouldn't indulge themselves in a free fight.

What impressed those who hankered after a little action most was the way no attempt had been made to cover up the fight, as it would most certainly have been covered ashore, by the old hands. They shared the skipper's views. You could fight one another to your heart's content in harbour, but at sea there were only two enemies, the damned English and the sea itself. Or three, if you counted the mindless boredom of it all.

Wolz did not often allow boredom to master him. He stared up at Willi again and then the report they had all been waiting for flowed down the line.

'Ship in sight – no, two vessels!'

Ludecke appeared on the conning tower with a white towel around his neck and dressed only in a pair of shorts. The men lounging on the deck vanished below through the hatches like a scurry of ants escaping down a crack in a lawn.

'One's a tanker.' Willi's handling of the kite betrayed him then and the water wagtail waggled her tail violently. When he had her under control again they were treated to a long series of curses, and then: 'Ship and tanker. Hove to.'

'Get yourself down, Willi.'

The crew on duty began winching the Bachstelze in. Ludecke turned the head of the boat towards the sighting. The Bachstelze reeled in. Working at normal speed it would take twenty minutes to stow the kite away. Wolz prepared to watch as Willi superintended that operation, feeling rather pleased that he could observe loftily from his perch as Willi sweated it out.

Lucky, now, that he was on watch, after all.

He'd have a ringside seat for all the fun.

'There's only one explanation, Baldur,' said Ludecke, lowering his glasses. The horizon remained empty. 'That tanker must be English, and the *Rugen* must have captured her. What luck!'

Willi reported in and said the ship didn't look anything like what they'd expected *Rugen* to be.

'They disguise 'em,' said Wolz.

'Who'd be a surface raider?' said Ludecke. 'It must be like a tatty provincial theatre, all paint and canvas.'

'And nowhere to go in a storm,' said Willi, remembering what Ludecke was fond of saying.

Something prompted Wolz to say: 'Except straight to the bottom.'

The other two didn't exactly care for that.

U-42 approached the two ships carefully. The tanker rose high above the water, yet she was well-loaded. Ludecke cleared the conning tower and then dropped down the iron ladder – the early U-boats had had brass ladders, but brass was too much of a strategic metal these days – and slammed the hatch down.

'Periscope depth!' yelled Meisten.

The helmsman and the planesmen controlled the boat. The bubble barely moved. The hum of the electric motors sounded like a swarm of bees on a summer's day. The periscope went up and Ludecke peered, first twisting his cap around in that unnecessary but endearing way.

'No sense in taking chances,' he said, for Meisten's benefit. 'The tanker's English, of course, but we don't know if the other ship is *Rugen* or some damned English A.M.C. refuelling.'

Ludecke took U-42 in and checked more thoroughly. He saw the ship clearly, studying her closely. At length, satisfied she was *Rugen*, he gave orders to blow tanks. Like some prehistoric monster from the deeps, the U-boat blew and surfaced, the water sluicing off her casing and spouting out through the vents. Ludecke scrambled up the ladder and amidst a welter of spattering water-drops threw back the hatch and climbed into the conning tower.

As Officer of the Watch, Wolz followed. He took off his cap and wiped his hand over his fair hair, then put the cap back on. He drew out his silver cigar case and offered it to Ludecke.

'Celebration, Baldur?'

'Something like that.'

Presently, when contact had been made and the hands could come up and the warps were thrown and the boat nuzzled in carefully against the stern of *Rugen*, Wolz felt that, well, yes, this was something to celebrate. Although they were off the main shipping lanes, here were two units of the German Navy and a prize. Had he been given to over-sentimentality, he would have agreed that the moment was one in which German naval pride might ride high.

As it was, at Ludecke's order, he bellowed the hands into inflating and launching the rubber boat over the side. The Commander was going to pay his respects to Kapitan zur See Klaus Frohlich.

Ludecke had put on his blue uniform, the buttons well-polished, and set his cap at the jaunty submariner's angle.

'How do I look, Baldur?'

'It's a great pity there are no girls in the ship.'

'I might have known. You're worse than Willi.'

With that Kapitanleutnant Gustav Ludecke had himself rowed over to *Rugen*. He went up the side in fine style and Wolz saw him hand himself inboard and vanish. Wolz grunted.

'Now he'll have a stiff drink and see new faces and hear the news. It's very fine to be captain of a boat.'

'One day,' said Willi, going forward. 'One day, Baldur—'

'Yes, Willi. You're right. One day we'll have our own boats.'

The idea of commanding a U-boat had come to be the greatest single thing on Baldur Wolz's horizon. Even the thought of the swastika gently thumping the soft inside curves of Marlene's breasts, even Lottie's romping, faded by comparison. As for Lisl – well, she stood remote, in a different time, not a part of the real world at all.

Mind you, Wolz reflected as the thick hoses began to snake out, mind you, there were ideas to be contemplated regarding the Baroness von Hartstein's daughter, Trudi. If the bloody English minded their own business long enough for him to have his own boat, and carry out a few successful patrols and sail back with a full rig of pennons, he might be well in the running there, despite the Luftwaffe and Cousin Manfred, and the S.S. and Cousin Siegfried. As for Cousin Helmut; he was the middle son and what he did remained a mystery to Wolz. Helmut was powerfully built, and yet walked like a cat. He had damned fishy eyes – and he wore civilian clothes. Wolz did not wish to enquire too closely into what Helmut was doing for his war effort.

The hoses began to pulse, thick and oily, like umbilical cords. *Rugen* launched a longboat and between them the two crews began to ferry across the torpedoes. Four had been expended uselessly against that domineering British battleship, and one had reached orgasm with *Willowmore*. So five reloads would be in order.

As for the breech for the 10.5 centimetre—

71

'Nothing doing, Baldur,' said Ludecke, returning a little the worse for wear. He clutched the coaming, smiling, ready to forgive Kapitan zur See Frohlich for not carrying a spare breech for his gun. 'We'll have to carry on with the 3.7.'

Meisten, on deck and supervising in his cutting way the refuelling operations, made a face, and said something about typical lack of proper organisation ...

Here Ludecke dropped down the conning tower and Wolz decided it was time Willi relieved him on watch.

Down in the wardroom he said to Ludecke: 'Any chance of going across to *Rugen*?'

Ludecke eyed him a little owlishly. He pulled a bottle from his pocket and then, hesitating, handed it across. It was schnapps.

'What do you think we are, Baldur? A blasted pleasure ferry? There's a war on. Have a drink.'

Wolz did not hesitate. Schnapps was forbidden. But, what the hell, all skippers carried plentiful supplies and half the Navy functioned with the aid of spirits. No-one admitted it, no-one would mention it, but it was so.

'Job for you, Baldur.' Ludecke looked pointedly at the bottle, so Wolz took another good swingeing swig and handed it back.

'Yes, sir?'

'Stowage of torpedoes.'

'I might have guessed.'

'Cheer up, Baldur. You drew the fish to check the pistols in a mighty fine style. Mighty fine. I admired you. The hands will just have to clear their traps out of it, use the P.O.'s mess to stow things.' The for'ard mess deck was merely the for'ard torpedo room. 'And get the job done before dark. I think Number One will have topped up the tanks by then, if he doesn't get some idiot killed in the lines. I want to be clear of

Rugen and the tanker. Two damn big inviting targets.'

Ludecke looked a little owlishly at the bottle.

'Damned good stuff, this. Drink?'

Wolz let the level down a bit and then rolled up onto the casing through the for'ard hatch, yelling at the men to clear their gear out of the way. 'Men's work now,' he said, and stared solemnly at the boat pulling across with the first fish.

Everyone stripped off. The heat had been not quite intolerable and the lemonade was still in plentiful supply. Wolz just hoped Ludecke had requested plenty of lemonade from Kapitan Frohlich. Down in the guts of the boat the heat could hit over ninety-five, and then a man sweated rivers and needed plenty of water intake. If the water condenser should give out ... Well, Wolz was not one to worry overmuch about what might happen when it lay beyond his control.

As to loading torpedoes, though, that lay very much in his control. Every time they stowed torpedoes he thought of Rudi. Rudi von Falkensbach and Emil Zerbts, both harum-scarum midshipmen going through U-boat training like himself, as mad and wild and reckless. Even though Rudi was a von, he would never allow anyone to address him as, no doubt, his father the Graf would have wished. He was always Rudi to his friends. Rudi, a good comrade, laughing, joking, always with a case or two of good German wine from the estates, just for once allowing a tiny slip in the strict procedure, the torpedo slipping from the slings and the jeers collapsing, Emil with barely time to scream before the tinfish pulped him and turned him into a red pudding jelly on the casing. The blood ran out over the steel and the torpedo rolled over the side, dragging with it the chains and the slings and the crushed pulp that had been Emil Zerbts.

Torpedo stowage was a time when Wolz checked everything very thoroughly, and then started all over again and checked through even more meticulously.

Rudi von Falkensbach and Wolz had gone down to Mainz to see Emil's parents on their leave, their starched white collars cutting into their necks, and they'd made no attempt to explain exactly what had happened. In the Navy the fact of death was something you grew accustomed to. It was never pretty. There was no need to inflict details on others, particularly upon parents and sisters. Rudi had even left Emil's sister alone, feeling miserable. He'd been thoroughly down for months.

They'd tried to get posted to the same boat, but Base separated them, and now they met only on those occasions when fate decreed their boats were in together – which was not frequent. All the same, for Wolz, Rudi remained a firm friend and they corresponded regularly, and swapped tall tales, and tried to keep track of the rest of the class. Some of them had already been killed, even before the war.

So what with the heat and the sweat – and now the U-boat stank as much of sweat and mouldy leather as of pitch and sea-water – and the torpedo stowing and the care he exercised as a kind of religious rite in memory of Emil, Wolz worked up a tremendous sweat and a terrible thirst.

Most of the men had a sweat rash of varying degrees of severity, and some were already sprouting pustules under their beards. But they worked with a will, for the buzz was out that *Rugen* had sent across fresh meat and vegetables from her refrigerated stores. And (a word passed from the side of the mouth from one to the other) the news that Machinist's Mate Oberdorf had swapped something unmentionable for a crate of beer. The beer came across camouflaged. Wolz wondered what Ludecke would do – he knew what he himself would do – but he looked up to the Commander and attempted to model much of his own behaviour upon his. Meisten, somehow, didn't seem to have heard about the beer

'Look at Daddy!' said Speidel, hauling at the chains. He spoke quietly to the Cox'n, and Goehle, looking up at the bridge, said something about his oath and then a tart remark to the effect that Speidel needed to put his back into it.

For Ludecke had appeared on the conning tower brandishing a machine pistol. His white cap was tilted over one ear.

When Ruderman fell in the water that was Ludecke's excuse.

'Sharks!' he bellowed, and pointed the machine pistol past Ruderman's ear and let fly a full clip. The water was churned into a dancing spray of miniature white-tipped volcanoes. Ruderman seized the line flung by Goehle and clambered out as though a shark had been nuzzling his privates. He looked shaken.

'Was there a shark?' he asked everyone, looking about, shaking the water from him like some dredged-up shaggy dog.

They all laughed and mocked him; but he believed it.

Up on the bridge Ludecke slapped another clip in and bellowed down, generously. 'There'll be another shark for the next one in – and another clip.'

Well, they all knew Daddy when he got into this kind of mood.

Meisten showed his contempt for the skipper by ostentatiously lighting a cigarette and going off for'ard and hurling the cigarette into the sea before he got anywhere near the oil hoses.

'Damned party swine,' someone said, but low, out of hearing of the officers.

Wolz leaned against the conning tower. He watched *Rugen* and wondered what life would be like in a surface raider. The men waiting for the next torpedo lounged about the casing. They were a feckless bunch, given their trade. Ruderman, the fellow his comrades called the sick-berth attendant, kept on about his adventure with the sharks. Goehle sat reading an old magazine. Speidel leaned against the conning tower, glancing askance at Wolz as the Leutnant extracted his silver cigarette case, and put a thin black cheroot between his teeth. Wolz lit up and dragged on the smoke, watching *Rugen*'s longboat pulling across the water between the two vessels, going wide.

The longboat was carrying cases of 2 centimetre ammunition for the two flaks and 3.7 centimetre for the aft gun. The torpedo lay between the oarsmen, long and gleaming and lethal.

Wolz saw the flare of the explosion just as his mouth filled with smoke.

The longboat vanished in a ghastly eruption of smoke and flame. Bits and pieces flew up. He saw a man, ripped like a rag doll, going up cartwheeling, his arms and legs spinning.

The noise blasted at him.

He heard a squashy clanging thunk by his head, and swung around, shaking.

Speidel's face betrayed nothing. Shock, no, horror, no – nothing. But his head rolled off the red pulped mass that was all that was left of his chest. His legs collapsed and fell and rolled grotesquely over the side. The obscene mass of red pudding that was his chest fell sideways, his arms flapping.

A chunk of metal, a part of the torpedo probably, had flown with murderous accuracy. It had pulped Speidel's torso against the hard steel of the conning tower, clanging through flesh and blood and bone.

Wolz stared in sick horror as the refuse that had been a man slid wet and dripping over the casing into the sea.

Speidel had been standing close – close.

Another few centimetres for'ard and it would have been Baldur Wolz and not Speidel. It would have been

Wolz whose crushed and blood-spouting body slid over-side. It would have been Wolz's head that rolled like a crimson-dripping football along the casing and then gently trundled off into the sea.

Wolz turned away. He felt the revulsion, the nausea. Ludecke was yelling.

Bits and pieces from the explosion scattered down and clanging against the U-boat ricocheted into the water.

A spreading white circle of churned-up foam marked the spot where the longboat had erupted. Gun am-munition, probably, for the eel had the primer re-moved.

Whatever it was, the accident had happened.

Accidents were always happening. Rudi von Fal-kensbach knew that – now. Baldur Wolz knew it. Everyone knew it..

The men were chastened, shaken by the suddenness and violence of the tragedy.

Presently, normal life resumed, the ringing echoes of the explosion could be expunged from the men's ears. But the sight would not leave their minds for some time; the knowledge of comrades blown to pieces would stay with them.

The risk of being killed by accident in front-line action was something the U-boat men shared with their comrades in all the fighting services. The next torpedo would come across; nothing had changed.

Although after the accident the torpedo stowage went well, the boat was finished with taking on oil long before she'd finished with gulping down fish.

The sky took on that bruised, plum-coloured look. The sea remained calm, with a long oily run to it, and over to the west the sea and sky burned in long lemon-coloured streaks. Clouds floated like archipelagoes from a fairyland that knew nothing of war and death.

A signalman on *Rugen*'s bridge began flapping his flags. The boat's signaller answered and then called out the message. Kapitan Frohlich wished to suspend torpedo-loading for the night and resume in the morning.

Ludecke, his hat precarious, his face shining, but in full command of himself and his boat, agreed.

'Dinner,' he said.

So the boat settled to night routine and the watches changed and life went on in the mid-Atlantic. Just before dawn Ludecke crawled up to the bridge. He did not say good morning to the Quartermaster in the conning tower. He looked all about the horizon as the light grew. *Rugen* and the tanker, lumps of dark flotsam, gradually took on brighter and brighter images against the radiance flowing up from the eastern horizon.

'Damned odd, when you think about it,' said Ludecke.

'Quite right, sir,' said Wolz, chewing on his cigar which was unlit.

'The sun, I mean. We saw it vanish last night, and now here it is again, rolling up on the other side of the world. A damned tricky customer, the sun.'

The delay had cost them the best of the weather.

Mist hung in patches over the water, which had a leaden hue. As the last of the torpedoes was ferried across a rain squall drove down, wetting everyone. The men relished this. The water was rain water, fresh water, and did not cake in the cracks in their skin and drive salt deeply into splits and cuts.

Wolz took his usual meticulous care over the torpedo. The hands made sarcastic comments about him, but not when he might hear. They had all cultivated a lively sense of respect when it came to the second watch-keeping officer. They understood he knew his business – well, that was expected. But they understood, also, that he could handle not only the men, but himself. Wolz did not feel it incumbent on himself to disabuse them.

With the last fish safely stowed the men started to bring their gear out of the P.O.'s mess, not without a few ripe remarks bandied about. Willi had the watch. The Chief pottered over his engines, for the port M.A.N. had been dicey and spurting too much and the stokers resented getting fire spat in their faces when they didn't expect it. Ludecke climbed up onto the bridge and settled down.

Rugen signalled one of those conventional messages sent at sea, full of good luck and good hunting, and Ludecke, with a straight face, authorised a similar reply. The tanker got up steam and set off towards the north-east.

'D'you think he's got a hope in hell of getting through?'

'Well, Willi, if the English don't sink him it's a good chance another U-boat will.'

Just then Wolz was sitting in the wardroom balancing a cup of coffee in one hand and trying to read a cheap erotic novel in the other, and finding neither much to his taste. The coffee was good, no doubt of that. The Navy called coffee of that particular consistency blacksweat; the ersatz stuff already in circulation at home bore no comparison. The U-boat Service received good food, there was no denying that.

Then he was sitting on the deck and the coffee had splashed all over the book.

The boat shook, as a dog shakes itself after a dip.

Men yelled. Another almighty crash sounded from outside.

Wolz scrambled up and ran through the hatch of the watertight door into the control room. Willi was down. The Chief was ready to flood, vents cleared. The sound of Ludecke yelling: 'Flood!' and then the clang of the hatch were drowned by the hissing bubbling of compressed air.

The boat tilted down sharply by the bows. Down through the water she plunged.

'Blow fast-diving tanks! Stand by! Bring her up to thirty metres.'

The boat levelled off.

Wolf saw Meisten looking at the skipper.

'Gentlemen,' said Ludecke. 'We have been blessed by an Armed Merchant Cruiser. He had the effrontery to fire two shots at us.' He cast his eyes up, as though in prayer. 'Now we shall ascend and put a fish into him, and thus regain our dignity.' He snapped it out. 'Periscope depth!'

The Chief took the boat up. Ludecke twitched his white cap backwards and said, fiercely: 'Up periscope!'

CHAPTER EIGHT

The two men who had only been wounded by the six-inch shell from the Armed Merchant Cruiser were patched up by Ruderman, who now harboured an unexpressed horror of sharks. He had taken a five-day course in medical attention, so the others referred to him as their sick-berth attendant. Nothing could be done for the two men who had been blown to pieces. No doubt, had Ruderman cared to dwell on it, portions of their shattered anatomies were going into the daily diet of his pet sharks.

'Slow ahead both. Hold her steady, Chief.'

Ludecke swept the glass eye of the periscope around the horizon. *Rugen* looked a mess. She was on fire amidships and her dummy funnel fell in a mass of flames and sparks. But she continued to shoot.

The A.M.C. looked immense, towering up, with her funnel rearing to the sky. But Ludecke could see clearly enough that she was an elderly lady pretending to be a warship. Her six-inch guns spat with commendable speed. But the 5.9's of *Rugen* spat back, and even as Ludecke watched a gout of chips and splinters soared up from her boat deck. When the smoke cleared two of the boats were hanging in the davits and the flicker of a small fire showed, uncertainly, but growing .

'Down periscope, steer three-four-oh.'

'Steer three-four-oh,' repeated the helmsman.

Willi was hopping about from one foot to the other, but he had nothing much to do. The speeds and courses were laid out on the tracking table as Ludecke called them off. At times like these it was best just to watch and wait and learn all it was possible to learn against the time when you ran your own boat.

Only Ludecke was looking through the periscope. Now he said: 'Down periscope,' and then stood quite still, looking at his watch. His lips did not move, but they all knew he was calculating out the elapsed times. Meisten did his own job with a calm, almost contemptuous expertise. Wolz found he cared even less for the fellow than usual. Throwing that cigarette away like that – it was like smacking Daddy around the ears.

When the periscope went up the next time they all knew by the way the skipper tensed and then relaxed, letting his arms sag deliberately to control himself, that the A.M.C. had done something unexpected.

'Steer oh-seven-oh.'

'Steer oh-seven-oh,' said the helmsman.

Wolz pictured what was happening above. Ludecke was again absorbed in his mental calculations. Then he went over to the chart table and tilted the light and peered down like an eagle looking down from its eyrie over the territory it controlled.

Up there the English merchant cruiser had turned away, giving the U-boat no chance to shoot. They were well aware a U-boat was in the vicinity; they had shot at it. Wolz took some comfort from the well-known jumpiness of the English when U-boats were around. He wondered how *Rugen* was faring.

Ludecke carried his boat through a number of evolutions. Everyone knew he was stalking the A.M.C. up there. She was also well aware, as they knew, that she was being stalked.

At last Ludecke, with a final look through the 'scope, said: 'Down periscope. Steer one-nine-oh. Full ahead both.'

'Steer one-nine-oh,' said the helmsman.

'Full revolutions!'

The Chief began his famous coaxing act, persuading the electric motors to drive U-42 at a full half-knot better than her designers had ever imagined the boat would ever do.

The hydrophone operator had to concentrate. He sent in his report: 'Propeller effect increasing bearing one-four-five.' Then: 'Underwater explosions – bulkheads breaking—'

'Steer one-four-five.'

No-one needed to be told, now, what was happening.

'Prepare tubes one, three and four,' said Ludecke.

The orders were given. The tubes were flooded and the bow caps opened. The Chief Torpedo P.O. reported tubes ready.

'Up periscope.'

This time Ludecke took the attack periscope. He had ignored the tracking table for some time. Now, as they all waited, held rigid with expectation, they understood by his orders that it was going to be all right.

Wolz glanced at Willi. Willi looked exalted, lifted-up, his face compressed with inner emotion. Meisten just looked as though he was preparing to enter a rally at which the flags would wave and the speeches be made and the march past the saluting base would give him a fine view of the Presence.

'Salvo,' said Ludecke. 'Ten-second intervals. Loose one, three and four.'

And then, after what seemed an interminable wait: '*Loose!*'

Captain's Steward Alf Perkins shoved the tin hat back straight on his head and blew out a great gust of air. Blimey! That had been close. His steel helmet never really wanted to stay straight on his head, and the webbing strap never did seem to hold it firm, unless he fair choked himself. Now he clung onto the starboard bridge wing-rail and hauled himself up.

That brick had gone clean through the funnel. Black smoke poured out. Some of the lifeboats had been smashed and there was a fire burning away somewhere aft.

He looked back into the bridge and saw the calm figures of the Captain and his officers, the Helmsman, the Yeoman of Signals. They didn't seem at all perturbed. Perkins looked back again, off to the starboard beam, and saw the Jerry with flames leaping out of him and smoke roaring up, coiling and twisting. In that inferno a long tongue of livid orange flame spat. Where the shell went Perkins had no idea.

He took a fresh grip on his Lewis.

Saltburn Head had run through a dissipating rain squall and there, bold as brass, lay the raider. A tanker was fast vanishing to the north-east. Perkins knew that once the skipper had finished with this Jerry he'd be off after the tanker like a ferret down a rabbit-hole. And that bloody sub! They'd shot at the beastly thing. Perkins had no idea if they'd hit it or not. But it was around somewhere, hanging about, like some vicious shark, dirty, underhand, waiting to slip a torpedo into their guts and drown them all without hope.

The noise sounded remote, as though it had no part in his scheme of life. The flames roared. The shells exploded. The guns banged. *Saltburn Head* turned on generous rudder, swung back, curved like a snake through the seas.

The gunners cursed the Old Man, but they kept their sights on the raider and pumped six-inch after six-inch into him. His dummy funnel burned out, and smoke lay in greasy streamers across the water. The white spume of hits along the waterline told them they were hurting him. A 5.9 inch shot into the air, barrel and breech and mounting turning like a lazy catherine-wheel. It splashed down into the sea between the two ships.

Someone on the for'ard deck by the second six-inch had a wet enough throat to yell.

Even Alf Perkins knew, having heard the P.O.s talking, that a modern German 5.9 inch, what the Jerries called a 15 centimetre, was miles better than these old British six-inchers, that should have been pensioned off before Jutland. But the Gunner knew his business and was reaping the benefit of harsh words to the gun crews. The British six-inchers were chewing up the raider.

And *Rugen* hit back.

Perkins felt the jar through his feet and to his surprise was lifted quite nine inches off the deck. He landed with a thump. He had not let go his death-grip on the Lewis. Harry Bell, the number two, lay on the deck below with what was left of his head dripping red oily streamers into the scuppers.

The next Jerry brick hit aft and *Saltburn Head* slewed wildly in the sea. Her guns tracked aft across the bearings as she turned, keeping up their rate of fire.

Captain Manning got the report.

'Rudder jammed, sir.'

'Clear it as fast as you can, Number Three.'

'Aye aye, sir.'

The men worked feverishly to clear away the thick plating bent and twisted over the rudder head. It was a job calling for strength and skill and application, with the ship heaving through the water, for the Skipper wouldn't slow down with a U-boat in the vicinity. The heat smote them. The fumes blew back from the fire and choked them. Water slapped into their faces. But they struggled on and freed the jammed gear.

Perkins gripped the butt of the Lewis and wished that they'd get in close enough for him to have a squirt. He felt convinced the raider would sink soon without any help from him. He wondered only once why he'd been left on the bridge wing during action; but common sense, which you had to develop if you worked in a caff in Stockwell, soon told him the answer.

Saltburn Head shook herself as the jammed rudder freed and lurched over onto the other tack. Now the

85

portside guns could come into action. They took up the challenge, the crews sweating away, feeding the insatiable breeches, the smoke and fumes blowing back, the livid tongues of flame shooting out, and the crash and bang and recoil juddering through their nerves.

'She's going!' someone yelled in a crazy moment of near-silence.

The flames crackled up afresh and the working parties handled new hoses, for the old had been shredded by shell splinters, and started to douse down the fire.

The raider was going.

'Cease fire, Guns,' said the captain.

'Stop, stop, stop,' said Guns, and looked very pleased with himself.

'You can grin' said Captain Manning. 'Next time make sure you get the U-boat.'

'Aye aye, sir—'

Saltburn Head turned as *Rugen* sank. With the U-boat known to be around, the men in the sea must take their chances until one or the other decided the issue. Manning knew only too much about *Cressy*, *Hogue* and *Aboukir* and U-9. Those names were engraved on the hearts of every big-cruiser man. He gave a calm order which, because he felt it to be necessary, revealed the depths of his feelings.

'Make sure the look-outs keep their eyes skinned, Chief.'

'Aye aye, sir,' said the C.P.O. As Chief Yeoman of Signals he'd do more to his look-outs if they didn't keep a weather eye open than all the bloody U-boats in Creation.

He took his big telescope and went out to the bridge wing where Perkins gripped the Lewis.

'If you don't want your most sensitive areas knocked off, Perkins, keep your eyes skinned. There's a U-boat out there.'

'How's the fire, Chief? Shall I—?'

'You stay here and keep a look out! I'll tell you what to do.'

The Yeoman took himself off to the port side. Perkins pushed his tin hat straight and looked from for'ard to the beam, and then started over. Next time he looked aft of the beam as well. *Saltburn Head*'s bows swung around and Perkins could see the last moments of the Jerry. Her flag still flew. She went down by the stern, and her bows stuck up perpendicularly. Water boiled away from her. Perkins could see no survivors on any part of the wreckage, but dark dots spattered the sea near her, and a few life-rafts floated, like blackcurrants and buttered bread with blackcurrant jam. He looked around his sector, religiously, for the betraying white spume of a periscope, and saw nothing, and looked back and the raider was gone.

Saltburn Head straightened up and Captain Manning said: 'Thank you, gentlemen. A briskly-fought action. Now we must get after the tanker. Steer oh-four-five.' He looked around his bridge and although he did not smile it was clear to them all he felt a very proud and lucky man. Most of the bridge party just considered themselves extraordinarily lucky to be still alive.

Captain Manning exchanged a few words with the Chief Engineer. 'And we'll have the funnel patched in no time, Chief. Just give me all you can.'

'Ye'll get what these poor auld engines can give, skipper, and then, mebbe, a wee bit more.'

Saltburn Head began to turn, swinging her bows from her last course to settle down after the tanker. And as she swung so Perkins, peering through his glasses, saw a tiny black object sticking out of the water, with a white spume training away aft. He was sure it had not been there a moment ago ...

He shouted.

'*Submarine!*' Then, as he had been taught, he bel-

87

lowed off the bearing and range, as near as he could figure it, the bearing from the card, the range from sheer guesswork.

And then, he felt everything still and slow down, as though the film had broken in the pictures back home. He took a breath.

'*Torpedoes running!*'

Saltburn Head was still turning. Captain Manning appeared on the bridge wing, leaning over, craning to see as the ship turned. Across the sea three white streaks furrowed the water. As Perkins stood at the captain's elbow he saw the streaks just under the surface of the water. He tried to swallow and could not. Sweat trickled under the leather band of his tin hat. His eyes stung.

Manning said, crisply: 'Let her swing. The fish will miss.' He saw Perkins, and said: 'Something wrong with the Jerry torpedoes, Alf. Too near the surface, and they're curving off course. Nothing to worry about.'

The A.M.C. swung her tall hull through the sea.

Perkins licked his lips.

The captain looked aft. Now it was clear the torpedoes were veering off course for the ship. They would run aft.

'Close, though,' said Manning, and he let air escape through his clenched teeth.

The torpedoes ran into the disturbed water in *Saltburn Head*'s wake. She turned and kicked the water from her twin propellers. The torpedoes blew up in the wash with loud explosions. White water spumed into the air. The ship shook. Everyone jumped. And then the A.M.C. was sailing along as though nothing had happened

Alf Perkins looked at the captain. Manning stared across the tumbled sea and his brows drew down. His lips clamped.

Then he walked back to the bridge telegraphs.

'Stop both,' he said. 'Gun's crews stay closed up. The

88

blighter will come up to look at us. Then we'll blow him out of the water.'

Alf Perkins found he could swallow again. It hurt.

As the throb of the engines died he found himself wondering what the U-boat skipper would do if he didn't come up. He just wanted, speaking personally, to get out of here as fast as possible.

Captain Manning, quite calmly, said: 'Go easy with the fire. Keep it under control, but let plenty of smoke about along the boat decks. Oh, and swing out a couple of the undamaged boats. Don't lower away though. Tell off a party to prepare to board.'

As his orders were carried out he went to the port bridge wing and looked thoughtfully out. When he came back again he had himself under control. He knew the chance he was taking. Not for himself, not even so much for the old *Saltburn Head*, but for the men under his command – they were the loads upon his conscience.

But he had faith enough in himself and his men to believe he was doing the right thing.

'Take her up,' said Kapitanleutnant Gustav Ludecke. 'Guns' crew stand by. Flak guns' crews stand by. Break out the ammunition.

There would be no 10.5 centimetre gun this time. Wolz prepared to dash up the ladder after the skipper. He wanted to see the A.M.C. sinking. By the rules of warfare they would have to do what they could, even if the ship was a Navy unit.

U-42 lifted up through the sea. Her bows broke through in a smother of foam, water ran and belched from her, shining along the casing and breaking away from the conning tower. Ludecke had the hatch open and was on the bridge in an instant. Wolz bustled through after him and stared eagerly. The British ship looked huge, looming against the overcast. A fire sent up clouds of smoke from her aft superstructure, and boats were being swung out. She looked in a mess.

She did not appear to be listing to any degree.

The rest of the bridge party came up. Wolz swung down past the wintergarden towards the 3.7 centimetre. The crew followed. Meisten appeared beside the Skipper and they both trained their glasses on the British A.M.C.

Abruptly a great mass of black smoke belched from her funnel and poured from the shell-torn rents in the side.

The ship's head lay towards them.

She began to move through the water, to swing to port.

'She's not sinking!' screamed Meisten. He turned furiously on Ludecke. 'You missed!'

'You heard the explosions yourself! There's no time to argue now, Number One. She can't bring her guns to bear yet. Clear the bridge. Guns' crews below—'

'You won't have heard the last of this, Commander!' Meisten's face showed a yellowish tinge, and his eyes glared. 'Our duty to the Führer demands—'

'Clear the bridge!' bellowed Ludecke. 'He's trying to ram!'

Wolz bellowed his guns' crews inboard and saw them vanish down the ladder. He pushed past Meisten without a word. The A.M.C. was still turning. She looked enormous, slab-sided, towering, with that tumultuous mass of black smoke vomiting from her perforated funnel.

He dropped down the hatch without looking up. In seconds Meisten and then Ludecke would drop down and the hatch could be slammed. After that, when they'd flooded and were comfortably at periscope depth, they'd try number two fish and see what that could do. No stupid British A.M.C. was going to ram U-42! Daddy wouldn't allow that.

'Prepare to flood!' shouted Wolz.

The Chief responded in his usual way, without fuss.

Wolz looked up at the round whitely-lit opening of the hatch. In the next instant Meisten and the Skipper would drop through and then they would see about finishing this pestiferous British imitation cruiser for good and all.

'Confound the damned fellow!' said Captain Manning with commendable restraint. 'Either he's the biggest fool alive or he's born lucky.'

The U-boat had surfaced just ahead and not a single one of *Saltburn Head*'s six-inch guns would bear. They had been mounted on the beam and the for'ard pair would not depress sufficiently.

'Give me everything you've got, Chief!' shouted Manning down the voicepipe. 'Hard a-port, quarter-master!'

Sluggishly, the ship began to turn.

Alf Perkins could see nothing. He peered over the side of the bridge wing, craning, hanging onto the Lewis. The sub was out there somewhere – yes! There it was – a long dark streak on the water, like a crocodile, or a floating log. Then the conning tower came into view. He saw figures moving, men running, men disappearing like devils through a stage trapdoor. His mouth was abruptly wet. He lifted the butt of the Lewis and snugged it into his shoulder. The cocking lever snicked loudly. Just aim and squirt, the leading hand had said.

'Not enough speed to ram,' said Manning. 'Hell and damnation Turn, you old bitch, turn! Open fire as soon as the U-boat bears! And make sure you hit the bastard!'

Alf Perkins heard the repeated command. 'Open fire!'

He pointed the Lewis at the U-boat's conning tower. He could see a white dot over there. He pressed the trigger.

The double-drum jumped around. The gun shuddered. Smoke blew back. Perkins held the gun as steadily as he could, letting the whole drum of .303 go squirting up the tube. He pressed the trigger and the gun roared and bucked until, suddenly, there was silence. He didn't know if he'd shot the whole drum off or if the gun had jammed.

'She's submerging, sir!'

Manning danced with rage.

Saltburn Head was swinging with the force of the screws hammering her hard-over rudder. But before the six-inchers could come anywhere near the U-boat, she dived. They put four shots into the sea, wasting the taxpayer's money. Then there was only a spreading white whirlpool on the sea, and no sign of the boat at all.

'Full ahead both!' Manning shouted down the voice-pipe. 'Chief! Take us out of here – fast!'

The answer reassured him, for the Chief had a salty way with him. *Saltburn Head* swung and then steadied and showed her stern to that rapidly dissipating whirl-pool in the water.

No chance to ram now. The U-boat would have dived deep. If the A.M.C. hung about there would be only a watery grave for her company. And the tanker was drawing away farther and farther and she was a prize he had to take back.

Captain Manning did not know if it was sheer fool-ishness or blind luck that had saved the U-boat. But he felt highly chagrined. As *Saltburn Head* settled down to catch up with the tanker Manning consoled himself with the reflection that if he did his duty and fought well then the gods of war and goddamned luck always had the last say.

Captain's Steward Alf Perkins was speedily roused into realisation that just firing the Lewis gun was not the end of it.

'And make sure it's clean, Perkins! Clean, bright,

and slightly oiled! I don't want to find a single spot of dust anywhere! Lively, now.'

'Aye aye, killick,' said Alf Perkins, and wondered if he'd have time to fetch the skipper's kai before or after he cleaned the Lewis gun. With all the extra work, he had half a mind to wish he'd never fired it at all.

Baldur Wolz heard the distant tick-tocking as he stared up at the round opening of the hatchway waiting for Meisten and Daddy to come down.

He stood looking up, his face raised.

Wet drops fell down onto his face. He wiped them away and then stared at his fingers. They were red.

Instantly, he started up the ladder.

He put his head through the hatchway.

Daddy lay crumpled, with blood streaming from under his white cap.

Meisten was draped over the coaming. The back of his head was simply a great red hole, oozing.

'Below there!' bellowed Wolz. 'P.O. Get up here. Help me with the Commander.'

He hauled Ludecke to the hatch and levered him around so that his feet dangled. The control room P.O. came up and took the Commander's legs. Wolz more or less let Ludecke drop away below. He straightened up and pounced on Meisten. He took the Number One by the collar of his coat and by the seat of his trousers and hurled him over the coaming into the sea.

The A.M.C. was still turning and he could see the muzzles of two guns appearing as she swung. Back at the hatch he could hear yells from below. He bellowed as loudly as he could:

'Flood!'

Then he dropped onto the ladder, gripped the hatch and slammed it down hard. The wheel spun. He paused for a moment, catching his breath. The hissing bubble of compressed air and water, the cessation of the thumping from the diesels, the electric motors' shrill whine – all these noises and sensations flowed over him.

'Thirty metres!' he shouted down and then clambered down the rest of the way. He did not drop from the ladder in his old reckless style.

'What happened?' The Engineer Lieutenant stared at Wolz. 'Daddy's been taken to his cabin – he's had a nasty crack along the head. Where's Number One?'

'Meisten's dead, Chief. Hold us steady at thirty metres. Be prepared to group in smartly. Close up for depth-charging.'

'Very good—' The Chief, clearly, hadn't taken it all in but he knew what to do in this situation, having been given clear orders. Wolz called to the helmsman: 'Steer oh-four-five.'

'Steer-oh-four-five.'

The A.M.C. would probably try to depth-charge them. If she did, then they'd have to ride it out. If she did not, then Wolz figured she'd be after the tanker. He rather wanted to have another go at the British cruiser.

He went through to the wardroom.

Willi crouched over Ludecke, a bloody bandage in his hand. The Commander's white cap, blood-spattered, lay on the deck.

Willi said: 'He's had an awful crack, Baldur. Bullet grazed his scalp. I don't know how badly he's been hit—'

'Get Ruderman in here. Let him staunch the bleeding and we'll make Daddy comfortable.'

'What happened? Number One—?'

Wolz told him.

Willi's eyes opened.

'Depth-charges?'

'Probably. But nothing's happened yet. It's my bet the A.M.C. is after the tanker. *Rugen* sank.'

The boat ran smoothly You couldn't tell anything of what was going on on the surface.

'We'll wait a while and then surface. Have to see about those fellows from *Rugen*.'

'Yes.' Willi looked at Ludecke. His face looked shrunken, and black circles were forming under his eyes. The bleeding wouldn't stop. The bandage was soaked.

Willi stared up at Wolz, leaning over the Commander's bunk.

'You realise, Baldur? You – you're in command, now.'

The strange thing was, Baldur Wolz had been giving orders and running the boat as though it was the most natural thing in the world; yet until Willi Weidman put it into words he just hadn't taken it in.

But, by God, he was in command, now!

CHAPTER NINE

Kapitan Frohlich had last been seen clutching his neck and trying to speak. Blood had been pouring out between his fingers and dripping onto his smart blue jacket.

The man who reported this to Wolz remarked how the four gold rings had glittered in the fire glow.

Then Kapitan Frohlich had pitched forward and fallen through the blazing deck of the bridge. The flames had shot up and completely engulfed him.

Of his other officers only a midshipman remained to be dragged aboard U-42.

A midshipman and ten hands. They were all that remained of the complement that had sailed from Germany with such high hopes.

Wolz had them sent into the P.O.s' mess, a haven of refuge for wounded ducks and something the P.O.s had to put up with. As soon as the men were fully recovered he'd allot them to watches and quarter them up for'ard among the torpedoes. Not a single stoker had survived. The men could stand watch on the bridge, at the least, for U-42 was now running shorthanded, and learn something of a U-boat man's life.

As for the signal to BdU, here Wolz hesitated, thinking cautiously.

A signal must be made, of course.

Admiral Donitz insisted on receiving immediate and fullest reports. By these reports he was able to plan his grand strategy, to concentrate when he could, to direct U-boats to sightings, in general to co-ordinate the U-boat onslaught against England's shipping. The news of the sinking of *Rugen* might not depress the Admiral as much as it would, say, Grand Admiral Raeder. Wolz considered that. Donitz's entire belief now encom-

96

passed the U-boat campaign. With more boats he could promise to strangle England, and quickly. The dispersion of effort into surface warships, he would say, weakened Germany's war effort at sea.

Wolz always took a keen delight in watching the great battleships and cruisers at sea; but Germany possessed her panzerschiffs, of which one, *Graf Spee*, had been gloriously sunk in action, and the new battleships were not yet ready. It was U-boats in the front line from the word go. *Scharnhorst* and *Gneisenau* had already been in action, and the A.M.C. *Rawalpindi* had been sunk and a deal of convoyed shipping had gone to the bottom. But for all the grace and beauty of the surface ships, for all their power and speed, they had to take a back seat to the U-boats. They must. Wolz could see no other direction for the war at sea.

So he had to think carefully about the signal he must send.

If he just signalled, baldly, what had happened, and said the Commander was hors de combat, Donitz was very likely to order U-42 home at once.

Wolz realised he did not much fancy that.

Here he was, the senior officer, with a U-boat under his command, and, by all the devils in hell, he wanted to savour the moment! He wanted to command U-42. He wanted to take her into action, and send the tonnages to the bottom, and build up a reputation – not just for himself but for a whole variety of reasons, including his father, and the German Navy, and honour, and sheer professional pride – the U-boat arm of the German Navy was the proudest, the most glorious – and also that which suffered the most casualties.

Blood and death and pride, a heady and combustible mixture.

But this was what his blood called for.

Finally he wrote out a simple message: '*Rugen* sunk by A.M.C. Oberleutnant z.S. Meisten killed in action. In pursuit of A.M.C.' He worked the chart position very carefully, for BdU might be able to vector another U-boat – say U-40 of which they had heard nothing lately – and then appended the code for the state of the weather and sea, standard procedure.

With a firm hand he put Kapitanleutnant G. Ludecke, making no attempt to forge a signature. When he handed the signal to the telegraphist the coding took care of details, but Willi made a face.

'Daddy will recover all right, Willi,' said Wolz. 'You'll see.'

'If he doesn't and he dies, you'll be in the soup.' Willi sounded depressed. 'It's not even in the log.'

'It's on my pad. When it's transcribed into the log it can be done whichever way the cat jumps.'

'The Commander's just got to pull around. It's up to us now, Baldur. You and me – and the Chief, of course.'

'We'll manage. And we have *Rugen*'s survivors to help.'

'All the same, the fish didn't sink the Englishman. And they hit. We all heard them.'

'They exploded all right. The pistols worked. But I can't see how they hit without sinking her – unless the English have stuffed their A.M.C.s with something – wooden casks, say – to keep them afloat.'

Willi looked even more morose and went off to roust out the men in the control room, keeping them on their toes, just to keep his hand in.

The thought occurred to Wolz that Willi looked upset because now between them they'd have to stand watch and watch. He daren't trust the midshipman from *Rugen* on the bridge of a U-boat. He decided to try to cheer Willi up. A long face was catching.

Yes, Willi was a good fellow but if Rudi was here now! Between them they'd have U-42 spanking along, the finest boat in the fleet. They'd trained together and got drunk together and chased girls together. Memory of that glorious Christmas they'd spent together with those two – what were their names? – made him give strict instructions that this Christmas was to be celebrated in the good old German way, even if the Commander was lying in his bunk unconscious. The crew thought a great deal of their Commander. His reckless ways in everything except the hazarding of his boat made them see him more in the round, as a man and as a commander.

So the Christmas tree was made from toilet paper and wire, with pocket-torch bulbs to light up. The sausages festooning the overhead like swaying bulbous stalagtites were raided. The galley would work overtime. As for the beer – Wolz almost decided to stamp down hard and confiscate it. But the amount was so small that it would not affect alertness and discipline, and he calculated out with some shrewdness the balance between hard authority, the blind eye so beloved of the English, and plain common sense in this tricky situation.

All the same, he did say to the Coxswain: 'It may be Christmas, but if any man fouls up on duty he'll wish he'd never been born.'

Signal in from BdU made no comment on *Rugen*, expressed formal condolences for the loss of the First Lieutenant, gave instructions for the patrol to be resumed.

Wolz nodded comfortably.

Ludecke regained consciousness and stared about him vacantly. Willi looked even more upset. The .303 bullet had left a long bloody graze across the Captain's skull. Ruderman cut the hair away and dressed the wound. He said, with how much confidence in his own judgement Wolz had no idea, that the skull was not fractured. Ludecke was given a sedative and everyone expressed the hope that Daddy would recover quickly.

Wolz shared that hope. All the same, he meant to

make what he could of the situation whilst it lay under his hand.

Not for the first time he found that vague dissatisfaction with some of Ludecke's actions oppressing him. He admired Ludecke as a submarine commander. Ludecke had spent a great deal of time in the Baltic training new U-boat men and his great laugh and his open-handed enthusiasm always created a tremendous impact. The crews regarded him with awe and with affection. All the same, and here Baldur Wolz felt rather like a mean-spirited cur-dog, all the same, there were incidents in the patrol which Wolz, had he been in command, would have handled differently.

Well, now he was in command.

Not until some of the initial euphoria had worn off was it borne in on him that all was not well with his new command.

At first there was only the odd strange look, the quickly-turned head, the low-voiced comment he did not catch.

Leutnant Helmut Bergman was without doubt a very fine engineer officer, but on one occasion when Wolz called for periscope depth Bergman failed to hold the boat steadily in trim. The periscope cut under once, twice, and then for a third time.

Wolz said, somewhat crisply, into the voicepipe: 'Hold her steady.'

'Very good,' said the Chief, and Wolz heard him lambasting into the control room.

There was an edge to the Chief's voice, as though Bergman was holding himself in check and not coming out straight with what he wanted to say.

Wolz, sitting on the saddle seat up in the kiosk, brushed that away. The Chief would do his job. He peered through the rubber-framed eyepiece and scanned all around. Sea and sky, sky and sea, and not the whisper of a sighting.

'Down periscope. Take her up – surface.'

'Surface.'

The tanks blew and the boat surged her lean steel length up from the depths into the Atlantic sunshine. Up north now the days would be short and there would be snow flurries over the leaden sea, and the temperature would be right down. Standing watch on the bridge would be torture. Yes, decided Wolz, bashing the hatch up and clambering up onto the bridge, yes, far better to carry out active offensive patrols here, even if the pickings were not so thick, than up in the North Sea at this time of year.

From all he had learned and listened to he had the prickly idea that this war would not be soon over. There would be many chances of targets, plenty of time to pile up the tonnages sunk.

And, if the winter weather was not too severe, then the temperate zones were far more comfortable than the fierce heat of the tropics for a submarine. Suffocating inside a U-boat was simply torture. The stink of diesel fumes, the mingled aroma of sweat and rotting leather, cooking and pitch and that strange dizzying sense of pressure because the high-pressure air-lines always seeped into the atmosphere in the boat, made a man's senses swim. Pressure had to be regulated by the valve before the hatch could be thrown back and the sweet fresh air pour through the boat.

The same brilliant panorama of sea and sky met his gaze. He swept the horizon. Bare. Not a wisp of smoke. Not a single masthead. Well. The tonnages would come sailing up over the rim of the world to be sent tumbling down to the bed of the sea. They would.

He felt absolutely certain of this. Great Britain depended completely on her overseas trade. Without ships she was dead. As U-42 penetrated into the shipping lane Wolz knew that if England still survived then her ships must pass before him. Must.

The next day passed without a sighting.

Willi's face looked as long as an English horse's.

The men ate their dinners and played Skat and no doubt they grumbled. Wolz was reasonably sensitive to atmosphere. He could feel once again that unsettling impression of events brewing behind his back, and whilst he fought off unease he tried to bring into focus just what was making him uneasy.

Ludecke regained consciousness from time to time, and then would lapse with a few mumbled incoherencies back into his slumbers. Wolz felt for the skipper. But, instinctively, he felt he was doing the right thing.

What, he would say, would Donitz have done in these circumstances?

Donitz would have pressed on in the effort to sink enemy ships. That was what mattered.

'All the same, Baldur,' said Willi as they drank coffee together changing watch. 'All the same, Helmut thinks we ought to report Daddy as wounded and then sail for home.'

'Did he tell you this?'

'Oh, no. Of course not. But it's pretty plain.'

Wolz sipped his coffee. The sun shone, the boat sailed on evenly, the water creamed back in satisfyingly white rhythms to either beam.

'Helmut is the Chief, he runs the technical side. I run the boat. I think that is reasonably obvious.'

'All the same, Baldur—'

'All the same, Herr Leutnant, I do not wish to hear this subject brought up again.'

Willi Weidman did not flush, but the lumps ridged along his jaws. He nodded, stiffly.

'Very good!'

But he hadn't liked it. He and Wolz were friends, weren't they? And now Baldur Wolz was allowing his position to go to his head. He would like to be a martinet, a disciplinarian, cutting his friends down to size. Oh, yes, Wolz was under no illusions as to the thoughts furiously scudding through Willi's head.

Absolute obedience to orders had been drilled into them .

This was the sure cornerstone of the prowess of the Service.

But, all the same, as Willi had so fatuously said, all the same, he had no wish to create friction in the boat. He was in command and he would remain in command. But there was no reason to alienate Willi more than necessary. So, with a feeling of smugness that he did not welcome but which nevertheless he recognized with some self-approval, Wolz said:

'I realise you do not share that opinion, Willi. You are as well aware as are Ludecke and I that the patrol must come first. Our duty is to sink enemy shipping. I know you understand that Ludecke would want us to continue the patrol. Once he is recovered and can resume command he can report his wound and let BdU decide. But, for now, we both understand that for the good of the Service we must go on as though Ludecke still commanded. Hein?'

Willi looked more nonplussed by this attack than Wolz expected.

'Well, Baldur – yes, you are the Commander now. I did think you were a little high-handed just now – but—'

'But that's all a part of it, don't you see? The Navy is the Navy. Our traditions are fragile. You and I know they would not allow any mention of the events at the end of the last war at Academy. The sailor's mutiny – all that didn't happen as far as the Kriegsmarine is concerned. We don't go back like the Army. And, unlike the Luftwaffe, we do not have Goering to speak for us. So we must make our own traditions and our own destiny.'

'Well—'

'So you see, to just tamely pack up now, merely because the Commander has had a crack on the head – no, no, Willi. It wouldn't do. Wouldn't do at all.'

And then, even as Willi Weidman opened his mouth – a somewhat bewildered mouth under the barrage – the look-out's yell pierced them.

'Smoke! Red one – oh!'

The glasses whipped up. Wolz focussed his Zeiss and stared. Smoke – yes! A smudgy cloud, black and gorgeous on the horizon.

'Now, Willi,' he said and the satisfaction in his voice could not be disguised. 'Now we start sinking our own tonnages!'

Just before the alarm sounded Ruderman, Muller, Bohm and Blaum were arguing much more than playing Skat. The crew space, cramped between torpedoes and piping and conduits, subjected to the merciless white glare of the electric lighting, dripping moisture, was as much a home to them as anywhere. But the argument waxed and the cards were thrown down and forgotten.

'The man's gone mad!'

'Not mad, Walther. There's a name for it—'

'Yes – power madness.' Ruderman rubbed his unshaven chin. 'I patched up Daddy and it's not right he should be left without proper medical treatment—'

'Listen to our sick-bay attendant! Since when have you been so humble?'

'Since I know what I know, you numbskull! Daddy should be in a proper hospital with doctors and nurses—'

'Now nurses I approve of—'

'Not swanning about out here in a U-boat where the only attention he can get is all I can give him. I know my job. But they didn't train me to deal with this kind of mess.'

The others sobered at this. The affection they all felt for the skipper warned them that Ruderman meant what he said.

'This midshipman we scooped out of the sea,' said

Walther Bohm, carefully. 'Maybe he would have a word with Number Two.'

Muller in his sharp Berlin way, said: 'He thinks he's the Commander, now, not the Number Two. Anyway, this Fahnrich won't have the guts to stand up against Wolz.'

'Well, something's got to be done,' said Ruderman, and then the alarm sounded and they scrambled to their action stations.

With his quick Berlin wit, Muller had the last word.

'You're the medic. You put Daddy on his feet again.'

U-42 nosed towards the smudge of smoke and, for the moment, her crew became once more a fighting team. But the darker lesions persisted, and every man's thoughts went to the haggard-faced, gaunt figure lying still and unconscious in the commander's cabin.

At Wolz's sure, incisive commands, the Chief brought the boat to the surface.

Her lean bows broke in a flurry of white water. Water spouted away as she lifted in the sea and her casing rose gleaming into the sunlight.

Wolz adjusted pressures and slammed the hatch back.

The gun crews streamed out and manned their weapons.

'Put a shot across his bows,' rapped Wolz. He studied the vessel and was not impressed. She was a broken-down old tramp, of about four thousand tons, with a single tall smoke stack and a tall bridge that appeared to wobble with age. She carried no armament.

'They're abandoning ship. No radio signals.'

'Very good.'

The water lapped at the ballast tanks. The sun shone. The sweat stood out on the men's skin. Wolz looked at the miserable old tramp and his own previous thoughts recurred to him. Yes, it was pathetic to have to sink this old swayback vessel. She was probably a survivor of the last war, gone through it without a scratch. Now she had met her doom. Small and insignificant as she was, she could carry cargo, and, ergo, must be sent to the bottom, vide Admiral Donitz.

'We'll pick up the Master,' said Wolz. 'Willi, slap a few into her waterline.'

'I'll blow a few heavy breaths at her,' said Willi, laughing, shielding his eyes from the sunlight. 'A few puffs should blow her over.'

The 3.7 centimetre cracked out.

The white water climbed lazily from the old side of the ship. Almost at once she began to take water and to list. By the time the Master had scrambled onto the casing only the upperworks and the tall ridiculous funnel showed above the surface of the sea.

The Master was soon dealt with. He could tell them nothing. His vessel had gone and he and his crew faced a long pull to the mainland. Wolz saw the English were provided for, giving them water and sausages and tinned fruit. He had to give them a compass and tell them the bearing to sail.

The two boats stood off and the men in them, surprisingly smiling, began to hoist scraps of sail. No one had been killed. A ship had been sunk. The tonnage successes of U-42 had increased by three thousand seven hundred tons.

'That makes it seventeen thousand one hundred tons, Willi. We're improving. But we've a long way to go yet.'

It had all, considered Wolz, been so easy. Just rising up before the startled tramp, a shot across the bows, the short wait for the crew to take to the boats, and then a few shots into the waterline, and bubbles.

Another pennant to fly from the periscope when they sailed victoriously back.

So, feeling through all his satisfaction those deep

and hurtful feelings of contradiction, Baldur Wolz went hunting more victims.

BdU signalled orders to close the West African coastline and attack shipping using the deep-water port of Port Bouin. Donitz had a bee in his bonnet that good pickings were to be had there. The advantage for the U-boat lay in the simple fact that shipping must converge for the port. Also, and Wolz nodded as he read the signal, Intelligence reported an almost complete lack of escort craft. England was stretched too much to allow of adequate escorts. Freetown to the south might be able to help; Cape Town was too far away, and Dakar could offer little. Wolz fancied BdU might be on to something here if they had inside information. Tankers were the prime target.

U-42 headed in for Port Bouin. Almost at once, during the forenoon watch, Wolz picked up smoke. He had not flown the Bachstelze because he expected shipping and he did not wish to spare the time for stowing the gyro-kite after a sighting. He gave orders and the Chief increased speed up to fourteen knots. U-42 thumped along over the surface until Wolz judged it expedient to dive.

He had attained a good attacking position on the port bow of the steamer. She was travelling north westwards at no more than seven and a half knots. The director angles would be perfect for a torpedo shoot; but Wolz knew too much about the confounded toothless wonders the Kriegsmarine had issued to their U-boats. He would trust to the 3.7 centimetre – as usual now.

U-42 eased up on her intended victim.

Climbing up into the kiosk Wolz straddled the saddle seat and said: 'Up periscope!'

He caught the handles and rammed his eyes against the rubber eyepiece.

A stumpy and ugly steamer, with a single funnel, rust-streaks along the side from the scuppers, a black hull, beige upperworks, the flag flying from the stern – he compressed his lips.

'Slow ahead on starboard motor only, Chief. One knot. Keep us in trim. Down periscope.'

Willi looked his consternation as Wolz clumped down into the control room. But at action stations he was held in the rigid stasis of discipline.

'Neutral,' said Wolz. 'Portuguese.'

Someone said something which Wolz refused to hear.

The men at their control positions looked sick.

'Secure from action stations. Keep her as she is.'

So U-42 sniffed along like a dog with his tail between his legs until the Portuguese was safely below the horizon. Then Wolz took the boat up again to resume the patrol.

This happened three times.

'Neutrals! Nothing but neutrals,' declared Muller, with great disgust.

Ruderman, desperately worried over the condition of the Commander, said with a flare of temper : 'A Jonah, that's what he is. A jinx – a hoodoo.'

The word passed.

Soon most of the hands referred to Leutnant z.S. Baldur Wolz as a Jonah. Nothing had gone right on this patrol. They had sunk three ships, three ships to a total value of tonnage sunk of seventeen thousand one hundred tons. The aces were sinking their fifty thousands, and everyone in the boat knew it.

Their torpedoes malfunctioned or did not explode. They had lost their main deck gun. Their First Lieutenant had been killed and they had lost valuable crewmates and friends. The Commander had been grievously wounded. And still this maniacal young Lieutenant insisted on continuing the patrol.

'Well,' Walther Bohm said, coming off watch, 'It wouldn't be so bad if we were sinking enemy ships. But there is nothing—'

'The Second Officer did sink one,' said Muller. His

Berlin smartness showed, now, for he prodded by his remark the expected reply.

'Of course! That was just a bait! He's brought bad luck and we're doing no good here. One he's got, as though someone was sorry for him on the English side. And now they're all laughing at him.'

But, for all their resentment, the hands were careful up to now not to allow Wolz to see how they felt. The general view was that they must persevere for a time longer. If their fortunes did not change they would have to put their heads together and think of their best course.

Mutiny was not to be thought of.

But there was no doubt that a disciplined U-boat crew could make the feelings of every last one of them known by the Commander. He could be made to see how the crew viewed his antics. Every last one could by his actions show his feelings, even the youngest of them all in the boat, young Hans, the Moses.

No commander could last if he did not carry his crew with him.

Willi Weidman tried twice more to speak to Wolz.

Twice Wolz was forced to place their relationship on the footing of Commander and Sub-lieutenant. He made amends subsequently, as he had done on the first occasion. But Wolz felt the atmosphere in the boat and knew he was on trial, that he faced the judgement of his fellow submariners.

He gave no credence to bad luck.

He knew why there were only neutrals. The reasons for that were obvious.

He brought U-42 in to lie off Port Bouin as the sun broke through over the distant coastline. Look-outs were posted. The instant a sighting was made, U-42 would dive and be in an attacking position.

Baldur Wolz was determined to sink his targets and pile up the tonnages until Gustav Ludecke was once more fit to take over command. Until then he, Baldur

Wolz, ran the boat. He'd deal so harshly with anyone who questioned his actions that they'd think themselves lucky to be still alive after he'd finished with them.

CHAPTER TEN

Lieutenant William Blakey, R.A.N., commanding H.M.A.S. *Ulmurra*, looked over the canvas dodger of his miniscule bridge and let rip a blinding series of colourful curses, finishing with: 'And stow that grin off your face or you'll be swabbing the heads out for a month of Sundays!'

A.B. Prendergast obediently wiped the grin off his face. But he, along with the rest of the *Ulmurra*'s crew, could not but be entertained by the sight of the young lady flying down the companionway and fairly hurling herself into the waiting boat alongside. She was, so they understood, the daughter of some businessman ashore in this Godforsaken spot where the heat took a man cruelly, and the water merely blasted the heat back at a fellow, all dripping and humid, quite unlike their native Aussie sunshine.

With the rapid departure of the boat for the green shore with its white houses and drooping trees and huddle of cranes and warehouses dockside, Bill Blakey could let rip.

He commanded this heap of rusted iron they called a minesweeping sloop, a relic of the Kaiser's war; they'd hauled him out of a natty little six-inch gun cruiser and a comfortable berth to run *Ulmurra* and clear possible mines that might be laid by problematical Jerry raiders or submarines.

Ulmurra had welcomed the sight of the lady, very trim in a white dress and a large-brimmed white hat, as she came aboard. What their Commander, Mad Bill Blakey, had been up to in the wardroom – they called it that and not a gunroom – they did not know. But whatever it was, Bluey swore blind she'd still been trying to do up the top three buttons of that white dress,

111

and Croc damned his feeble eyesight and said the skipper had got down to four buttons, and not one less.

However many buttons Blakey had managed to unlatch with his powerful fingers, he'd got nowhere with the lady, that was evident. The hands bent to their work about the deck, a never-ending tussle with the rust. *Ulmurra* was coal-fired and reciprocating-engined and should have been put out to pasture years ago. She was roomy in an inconvenient way, being of seven hundred and twenty tons displacement – or thereabouts, for some new equipment had been hastily added. She was two hundred and thirty-one feet long overall, with a beam of twenty-eight feet, and she housed seventy mortal souls living in sweat, humidity, heat, and the mingled odours of stale sweat, smelly socks, coal-dust, the rotting tang of vegetables and, sweat.

Seeing that the hands were hard at it, or as hard at it as they were ever likely to get, being tough Australian Navy, and hauled back into the Service to help out with old England's renewed punch-up with Germany, Blakey barged back to the wardroom. He was tall and powerfully built, with a leathery Australian tan, and eyes crinkled with peering over distances, at sea and up the Blue. He found himself a gin and drank it down with a sour expression.

A sweet little number, and she hadn't even given him the time of day. What else was there for a bloke to do out here, save go crazy?

The Hon. Roger Cruellen-Marriott came in, smiling his lazy elegant smile.

'Well, Sub?'

'All squared away, sir. The depth-charges should all be aboard by eight bells.'

'And what we're supposed to do with them ...'

'The flap is there's a Jerry U-boat hanging about.'

'Our best bet will be to give the beggar a wide berth.' Blakey eyed his second-in-command with his usual exasperation. The Hon. Roger Cruellen-Marriott preferred to be called just Mr Marriott. What he'd done to be chucked off the bridge of a spanking new Tribal destroyer and despatched out here to moulder away with a crummy rustbucket of an over-age mine-sweeping sloop run by a gang of crazy Australians, Blakey did not know. At first he'd resented Marriott. After a time he'd come to welcome Marriott's presence aboard. The Sub could navigate, no doubt of that. And in his lazy, ironic drawl he could make the tough Australian hands jump.

'I hear the fishing's been poor, sir,' observed Marriott, very casually. He sat down and picked up a three-month-old magazine, filled with pomp and circumstance about the 'silent service' and other rubbish.

'Fishing?'

Blakey's tone was distinctly ugly.

'So it seems, sir.'

Blakey knew very well what the damned impertinent Sub was talking about. Everyone had seen the sheila come aboard and everyone must have seen her depart. And he'd thought he was on to a good thing there. Daddy was so impressed by the Australian sailors. Too right Daddy was. It was for the benefit of his cargoes that poor old *Ulmurra* had to sweep the channels.

'Don't you have anything to do, Sub?'

Marriott was too long in the tooth for that.

'If we slip at high water we'll be through the channel by first light. The Port Captain's secretary claims there is a U-boat – well, you know how they like to romance, sir ...'

'And if there is a U-boat we'll go out there and blow it out of the water with our depth-charges and our hydrophones, is that it?'

Marriott remarked, very coolly: 'Or the twelve-pounders, sir.'

Blakey bashed out and on to the bridge to make himself unpleasant to whoever he could catch dodging. By God! He'd serve the Service, all right, and maybe, one day when they found out he was still alive, they might deign to post him to a decent ship – a destroyer, say, or an eight-inch cruiser. Something, at least, more like a warship than *Ulmurra*.

The sun leaped above the horizon, turning the whole world into a coloured chiaroscuro. Wolz rubbed his eyes and peered again through the Zeiss. The coast seemed to slumber in mist-enwrapped half-darkness one moment and the next lay vivid and bathed in light and colour. He saw the whole scene sharply lit, as in a lantern show.

'Steer oh-seven-oh,' he said, in that sharp, no-nonsense voice he seemed to be using habitually these days.

'Steer oh-seven-oh.'

The look-out kept his eyes firmly affixed to his glasses and the signaller occupied himself most busily. Baldur Wolz was no man to cross these days.

The tanker steamed purposefully out between the marked buoys, the channel there swept of any possible mines that might have been laid by German raiders or U-boats. Wolz wondered if *Rugen* had paid the cost of her operation to the Third Reich. He studied the tanker. A fine large vessel of a good twelve thousand tons. A most tempting target.

He did not lick his lips. But his expression would have put the breeze up any of his crew had they dared to look at him instead of busying themselves about their tasks. He studiously avoided any appearance of excitement in his voice.

'Clear the bridge. Prepare to dive.'

The watch disappeared below with commendable brevity.

One and one-fifth seconds per man. The whole boat

to have dived in fifty seconds. Well, they could achieve that if pushed. But Wolz adhered to Ludecke's dictum – so far. Practise crash diving, yes; get below in good order and discipline when there was no need for haste.

At periscope depth he used the tube sparingly. The tanker must come out through the buoyed channel. U-42 had encountered no mines. Wolz did not believe in taking U-boats through uncharted minefields unless it was a matter of life and death.

'Slow ahead both. Steer oh-four-five.'

'Steer oh-four-five.'

Now they had the tanker with the sun beating on her and standing out against the horizon. She moved through the water with a grandeur that Wolz could not allow in any way to affect his judgement. She was merely an enemy vessel and must be sunk. He read off the bearings as they altered and the courses and the attack table spewed out the results when he called for them. Willi was up to the work. He'd have to be, otherwise the Commander would want to know why not.

The fact that Willi was by way of being a friend had nothing to do with it now.

'Prepare to surface. Bring her up smartly, Chief.'

There was a risk in surfacing this close to land. But Wolz was as certain as he could be that the English had no aerial patrols worthy of the name hereabouts as yet. And his information was that escorts did not exist.

The boat surfaced in a smother of white water tumbling away as the conning tower broke free. Wolz led the rush to the bridge and the guns.

He saw the tall bulky form of the tanker. And, beyond the tanker's bow, he saw a betraying flicker of white.

For an instant he stood braced, the Zeiss to his eyes, staring in passionate anger as the bows of the destroyer burst into view beyond and ahead of the tanker.

The destroyer saw them. With a massive discharge of smoke from her funnel she slewed hard aport and crashed foaming headlong towards the U-boat.

'Dive!' bellowed Wolz.

The men on the bridge scurried below. This time there was no practice about it, no thought lurking at the back of the mind that a foul-up would bring only a reprimand. This time a mistake could cost them all their lives.

The destroyer was belting along. Her funnel smoke darkened the sky, streaming away aft like a black and ominous banner of war. Her bow wave creamed high.

Wolz bundled the last man down and dropped through the hatch.

He was yelling: 'Flood!' long before he had the hatch closed.

He dragged the heavy metal cover down hard. Water splashed inboard, soaking him. He spat water from his mouth and shook his head, clearing his eyes, and all the time he was spinning the wheel. The clips slammed home.

U-42 plunged for the depths.

'Close up for depth-charging!'

Now they would have to face the terror.

This was the dread of the U-boat man, and this they must face and overcome – the depth-charging and the fear itself.

'Steer three-one-five. Full ahead both.'

'Steer three-one-five.'

The whine of the electric motors mounted shrilly. The boat slewed across to port, cutting a right angle through the water. Wolz's brain ran through the calculations. He could not allow himself to become excited. His face reflected only an iron will, a deeply-seated conviction that he could outwit the destroyer skipper aloft who sought to kill him.

The English vessel must follow her line. She would be listening on her hydrophones for his motors. The hydrophone operator in the boat could hear the destroyer's engines – and now everyone could hear them. They pounded up, sounding like an express train racing through a station without pausing.

The men remained rigid, standing in stiff poses, and those who did not have to look at their gauges and dials all cocked their heads up, as though they could see the destroyer speeding past over their heads.

With a whirring beating that drummed through the boat the propellers passed overhead.

Now!

Wolz felt his heart beating in a heavy regular thump. His skin felt tight. He was sweating. He forced himself to look as though this was a mere nothing.

The first depth-charge cracked off, a deep and yet penetrating *kerrrump* through the water.

The boat shook – but only a little.

The next depth-charge came closer. The noise rattled everyone's brains. The U-boat shook with a sudden fierce tremor. Two glasses burst and water spurted. The control room seemed to rotate. The P.O. gestured and the glasses were replaced, the water inflow ceased.

The third depth-charge exploded further off, giving the boat a gentle kick, from a distance, as though to say, well, old son, we missed you that time.

'Steer two-seven-oh. Group down. Port motor. One knot. Silent routine. Report damage.'

The reports would be whispered. If any man made a noise during silent routine his life thereafter would be hell – if he lived to suffer.

They heard the destroyer's screws thundering away. She did not appear to be turning. Her speed would make that a difficult operation. The noise faded.

Then the propeller noises changed in that subtle way that men who spend their lives underwater can read and understand. She was turning. She was coming back.

'Stop motors.'

The propeller-effect grew. It strengthened – but its strength slackened.

The English skipper was losing his speed so as to hear better through his hydrophones.

Wolz turned as casually as he could and looked at the men in the control room. Not one moved. He could barely make out their chests rising and falling as they breathed.

The destroyer passed away astern. They heard three heavy crumps, distant harbingers of a death that had passed them by. For how long was a question no U-boat cared to ask, contemptuous – at the moment – of the answer.

'Group up. Slow ahead both.'

Gently, near-silently, U-42 crept away from the deadly destroyer.

When he considered they were safe, Wolz refused to allow himself the luxury of what he craved above all things. How easy it would be to order the Chief to surface! They could rise up through the waters and surface and throw back the hatch and gulp down the beautiful fresh air – and then the destroyer would be upon them as a terrier pounces upon a rat.

Wolz had spoken enough times to old U-boat commanders, friends of his father, trying to understand something about the father he had never known. They had told him of the tricks the English destroyer captains got up to. Wolz did not think the English would have been so foolish as to have forgotten what they had so painfully learned in '17 and '18.

So he waited, patiently, like a deadly animal in ambush.

They heard no more of the destroyer.

When he felt that now, at the least, they must be safe, he still waited.

Then, at last, he gave the order.

'Periscope depth'

They rose smoothly, for the Chief had been so busy he had been fully occupied with his own department, and trimmed off. Through the tube Wolz made a quick three-sixty-degree scan. Nothing. The coast was not visible. Nothing in sight.

'Surface.'

As U-42 shook the water from her and rose into the sunshine, Baldur Wolz was busily working out the best course to follow the tanker and sink her. The escort would depart after a certain distance, and that tanker was a prize.

He would have her.

That was certain.

'So there *was* a bloody U-boat, after all!'

'The Secretary had it right for once, sir.'

Mad Bill Blakey stared out over the canvas dodger across the glittering sea. The tanker steamed grandly on, drawing away. Africa sweltered just over the horizon and the thought of pulling into the harbour and seeing if he could coax the sheila into another trial – hell, this time she'd have to be kind to him – made Blakey resent even more that stinking U-boat and its attempts to get at the tanker.

'If we'd been equipped with asdic,' said Marriott, more by way of expiation than explanation and doing nothing to soothe Blakey.

'Yes, Sub, your Tribal would have fixed her and straddled her and we'd all go back to a round of gins. As it is we're here and we stick with the tanker.'

'Yes, sir—'

'Those damned U-boats,' fumed Blakey. Then a gutsy laugh, more a roar of vengeful fury burst from him. 'I bet we made him wet his knickers! By God! We nearly had the bastard.'

'He'll have logged us as a destroyer, sir.' Marriott, calmly, eyed this fearsome Australian. 'All the U-boat skippers call everything that chases them destroyers.

We were a topline destroyer then, sir, for a time.'

'Sarcasm, Sub, is a mortal sin.'

'Aye aye, sir.'

So the old minesweeing sloop *Ulmurra* chugged on over the sparkling sea. A signal was taken in ordering Blakey to continue to cover the tanker. The presence of the U-boat worried the high naval officers in their comfortable billets ashore. *Ulmurra* was all they had, and, by God! they'd use her to do these Jerries' business for 'em!

Roger Cruellen-Marriott stood his watch, and brooded across that sunlit sea. War and more war, the deadly game of hide-and-seek, with the lethal killers beneath the sea seeking to blow the lumbering merchant ships out of the water – well, it would all make sense one day. If that fine new tanker was kippered she'd go up like a torch. There'd be little hope for the men in her. How they managed to find men to man the tankers and the ammunition ships always amazed Marriott. It was bad enough snaking about half-drowned in a small ship, like his old destroyer, or *Ulmurra*, but at least they had the comfort of being able to hit back.

If the Jerries loosed off a couple of kippers – the German Navy called them eels, he understood – it would be all up for anyone in the way.

He sighed and gave a tug to his cap and checked again on the look-outs. No warning could really be expected. Not if the U-boat skipper knew his job.

There'd just be the explosion and the gout of white water alongside the tanker's waterline and then the sickening mushrooming blast of the big bang, and the fires, and the oil on the sea, blazing, and the men screaming ...

None of it was pretty.

Marriott decided, not for the first time, that he'd see about that chicken farm his father had spoken of, and this time he'd mean it. Getting himself chucked off the Tribal destroyer had been a silly move. But, if he was here sweltering away with a gang of crazy Aussies in a tin-pot little minesweeper that should have been pensioned off in '18, why, then, he'd put thoughts of the chicken farm from his mind and concentrate on the job. Whatever happened, he'd have a go at the U-boat. He could do nothing else.

Baldur Wolz stared down at the charts and his lips drew back. Yes. The tanker would follow her course to the north and west. U-42 had faithfully followed. Before the sun went down he'd spot her, and then he'd have her.

No doubt the skipper of the British destroyer thought he had sunk the U-boat. That was a common mistake. If all the U-boats claimed as being sunk had been sunk the shipyards would never have been able to build them all.

He gripped his unlighted cigar between his teeth and the tube of tobacco slanted up aggressively like the muzzle of an 8.8 centimetre flak gun.

He'd damn well do it, and then he'd have to think very seriously about making a report to BdU. The wound Ludecke had taken had incapacitated the Commander and time was running out. Just let him get the tanker. Wolz did not pray for that eventuality, but he devoutly hoped for it with all his being.

To be brutally honest with himself he had to admit that he had never entertained the remotest idea that Ludecke would be unfit for so long. A crack on the head, the .303 glancing off the scalp and although producing a lot of blood giving no serious concussion, he had thought, would not do Ludecke any permanent harm. But Ludecke slumbered on.

Just let him get this tanker, then he'd report the true situation.

Still being honest with himself, he knew that he had expected at the most a day's command of U-42. That, in itself, would have been bliss. Now the days dragged on.

BdU must be told. Then it would be Kiel again if they were sent through to the Baltic.

Being honest with himself was one of those little games Baldur Wolz liked to play against fate. He'd be honest every now and then, usually when it suited him. Now, with U-42 plunging along after an English tanker, racing the setting sun, he could afford to be almost ninety per cent honest with himself. He felt sorry for Ludecke. Of course he did. But the Commander had a very loose tongue. He made no secret of his attitude to the National Socialist Party and Adolf Hitler. He made Wolz's neck prickle with some of the things he said.

Germany was once more a force in the world. There was no answer to that. Admiral Donitz knew what he was doing. Baldur Wolz saw the vision ahead with some clarity. He knew with a hundred per cent honesty that he was dedicated to making that vision come true.

The look-out bellowed and Wolz trained his Zeiss around onto the bearing, a mere five degrees from the point at which he had expected the tanker to appear over the horizon.

Yes. There she came, steaming on with all the arrogance of a British ship with a British captain sailing what he imagined still to be a British sea.

Wolz chomped on his cigar.

The U-boats were leaving no doubt in anyone's mind that no seas were British seas. The day of British sea-power was over, that sun had set, and the new sun of the Kriegsmarine's U-boat arm was rising.

He heard someone climbing through the tower but he did not take the glasses from his eyes. Willi would want to have a good look before they submerged, achieved a perfect firing position, and then surfaced to shell this arrogant British tanker into a blazing hulk.

'Prepare to dive, Willi,' said Wolz. 'Have a good look at the fat fellow. We'll singe his tail for him.'

A hand rapped Wolz on the shoulder.

'Very good, Herr Leutnant. Now go below and resume your duties. I shall speak to you later. I am resuming command.' Wolz span about, the Zeiss falling to dangle from their straps.

Kapitanleutnant Gustav Ludecke stared at him with a face like a corpse.

'Clear the bridge!' Ludecke spoke with anger and bitterness. 'Get below, Herr Leutnant!'

CHAPTER ELEVEN

'Daddy's in a most frightful rage,' said Willi Weidman.

He spoke, considered Wolz as he dropped down into the control room, with far too much anticipatory relish. Willi looked as though he was a huge tomcat about to lick up a whole dish of cream. Wolz felt the hurt of that.

'Flood!' came Ludecke's order and then the hollow clanging of the hatch. The Chief snapped his orders. He, it was clear, intended to keep well out of the line of fire when Ludecke started in on Baldur Wolz.

The diesels cut and the motors grouped in. U-42 slid beneath the waters like the enormous steel shark she was, in very truth, deadly in her invisible power. Wolz relished the imagery. But up on the saddle seat the Commander was reading off the bearings and ranges and there was work to be done and Wolz must put all thoughts of what lay in store for him from his mind. He was a trained and disciplined professional officer of the German Navy. That alone was what mattered.

Ludecke brought the boat in gently. Wolz could imagine exactly what was going on. The tanker was booming along in the last of the light and Ludecke would be content to bring the boat up within easy distance. A single shot would be enough. Long before the sun sank with all the splendours of a spectacular sunset into the ocean, the tanker would blaze to rival all those natural radiances, would herself sink with a coruscating display of man-made sunsets.

'Twelve thousand tons,' Willi was saying. 'This will make nearly thirty thousand.'

The electric motors whined with their almost unheard thrilling, the air-pumps hissed and sucked, the water ran whispering past the hull. The smells had not yet built up to their usual thick fog. The sense of pressure remained, heady, electric.

'Up periscope!'

The tube slid up. Ludecke turned expertly. Wolz could imagine it all—

'Down periscope! Crash dive! Take her down, Chief!'

Ludecke's frantic orders produced a galvanic effect.

At the same time the hydrophone operator sang out that he had two sets of propeller effects, just on the limits. Wolz wanted to scream out that the fellow was far too late.

U-42 plunged.

Ludecke plummeted into the control room and slammed the inner hatch shut. His corpse-face looked ghastly. The white submarine commander's cap was still twisted back to front. He gripped his own Zeiss, and his hands shook.

'Destroyer! Right on top of us.'

'Where did he come from?' demanded Willi. They slanted their heads. Their eyes showed the whites as they stared up.

The racing sounds of propellers vibrated through the water, impinging on the hull like a giant series of buzz saws. Down plunged the boat. The Chief looked anxiously at Ludecke. The commander gave no orders to blow bow tanks. Down and down deeper plunged U-42.

Wolz held himself rigid. He'd have blown bow tanks by now. He fancied the destroyer racing above their heads would be the same fellow they had escaped from before. He'd clung on to the tanker. Special orders had called for that. Wolz was certain.

The waiting tortured them.

The first depth-charges blew vast echoing concussions through the water. Wolz breathed a sigh of relief. The bombs were not too close. The boat shook. But the sounds of the screws above their heads receded.

Ludecke stood half-bent, his head cocked. He looked strange.

'Blow bow tanks. Trim us off.'

The boat's sharp angle decreased. The noise of the tanks blowing sounded extraordinarily loud to Wolz. Up there in the listening cabinet the English hydrophone operator would be crouched over his instruments, straining his ears, trying to pick up the sounds of the submarine in the deep waters. Wolz felt the sweat trickle down his nose. He wanted to scratch his beard, but he forced himself to remain unmoving.

The boat levelled off and trimmed.

'One knot, Chief.'

Silent routine held U-42 in a grip of terror.

The propellers roared back.

A fresh pattern of depth-charges dropped.

Closer, this time. Close enough to rattle the boat. Close enough to smash a gauge glass and spray water across the control room. The P.O. silently organised replacements. The boat shook again. A giant hand seized her and smashed her fiercely from side to side.

The lights went out. The bulbs all burst. In the darkness Ludecke switched on his torch and shone it on the control room P.O.

'Screw in fresh bulbs.'

Wolz could feel his emotions as distinct and apart from himself. The boat sank through the water, shuddering, forced down by the depth-charge explosions. The depth meters were in darkness. Ludecke shone his torch on them and the Chief pulled himself up from where he had been thrown. There was blood on his forehead.

'Destroyer approaching,' sang out the hydrophone operator.

'What's the bearing?' Ludecke's voice made them all jump.

'Destroyer bearing oh-five-oh.'

'Hard a-starboard. Steer three-four-oh. Full ahead port motor.'

U-42 turned like a hunted animal, trying to evade by erratic twists the hungry onslaught of the hounds.

More depth-charges tumbled down.

The fresh light-bulbs blew.

The darkness came back, and the sounds of men breathing, of someone praying out loud quite unaware. The boat shook.

Ludecke's torch suddenly shone on the conning tower hatch.

Wolz bent over the Commander.

Ludecke lay on the steel deck, his eyes wide and unseeing.

Wolz took the torch from his hand.

U-42 rattled as though bounced between iron jaws. The water parted by the depth-charge explosions pressed her one way and as the unimaginable tons of water flowed back she was hurled in the opposite direction.

Men were screaming.

Wolz said: 'Blow main ballast.'

The Chief staggered. But he gave the orders.

The boat began to rise.

The men found more torches and switched them on.

'Report destroyer's bearing,' said Wolz in an ugly voice.

'Destroyer bearing two-five-oh.'

'Slow ahead both.'

'Slow ahead both.'

'Stop blowing. Chief, trim her off at periscope depth. And do it right first time. If you show the conning tower—'

'I'll do it right,' said the Chief.

The emergency lighting had at last been fixed.

In the pallid glow which made them all seem corpses, or ghosts from a forgotten age, Wolz looked around the control room. A man lay unconscious by the gyro compass. Another gripped his arm and screamed.

'Take him away,' said Wolz. 'Get Ruderman to put him to sleep.'

'Destroyer bearing three-six-oh.'

'Stop motors.'

'Stop motors.'

Wolz slammed the hatch back and climbed up to the saddle seat. The quartermaster looked as though he was more dead than alive.

'Up periscope.'

He took a single sharp look on the bearing and then yelled:

'Down periscope.'

He had seen enough. The destroyer was approaching, but slowly, as though unsure. No doubt they were still listening deep. Now if he could just get an eel to function properly . . .

U-42 cut through the water just beneath the surface.

The destroyer could not see her, but she could hear.

How long would it be before the momentum of her forward passage could no longer keep her conning tower submerged? Yet to start motors now would bring instant reaction.

'Up periscope!'

Again that single flashing look on the bearing and:

'Down periscope!'

The destroyer had slowed right down. She was trying to listen more closely without the interference from her own screws. This was a stalk. Wolz could not bring U-42 onto the right bearing to loose a torpedo. To open up would bring the destroyer down on them, they would have to submerge, and then the depth-charges would start again.

Once more Wolz said: 'Up periscope.'

This time he saw the destroyer limned as a black silhouette against the last glow in the sky. The sun sank. Before he had need to say down periscope the darkness swamped across the sea.

Wolz smiled.

He took out a long thin black cigar and stuck it between his teeth.

'Now, now we shall have him.'

The boat's shambles was being cleared up. The depth-charging had shaken them all. Men had known fear. Wolz found a detached aloofness, almost a coldness, in him at the memory of the depth-charging. He had wondered, and now he knew.

'Stand by—' he started to say, getting the boat ready to blow the destroyer out of the water, intending to loose a fan spread of four eels and so make sure as far as he could.

Ludecke appeared in the conning tower. His face looked green and white in the unearthly illumination.

'Get back to the control room, Herr Leutnant. I am perfectly capable of running my own boat.'

Wolz stared sickly at him. Ludecke looked awful.

'But—'

'Are you disobeying an order?'

'No. No, sir.'

As he climbed down into the control room Wolz found himself, not for the first time, wishing the U-boat designers had adopted the British system of having the commander in the control room with his attack team. That way, now, Wolz could have exercised some restraint. He shuddered at what he imagined the Commander might do. Ludecke was off his head. That seemed obvious. Yet he spoke and acted normally – when he was conscious. No-one in the boat would support Wolz against Ludecke. To think otherwise was lunacy.

Ludecke called down the course, range and bearing.

The attack table gave the answers.

'Prepare one, three and four. Stand by two.'

Wolz shook his head. With the unpredictability of the eels and the way the destroyer had been hunting them, four torpedoes would be better.

Presently, Ludecke said: 'Loose!'

The three torpedoes sped through the water.

The men waited, the three stopwatches held in grasping hands, in the torpedo room, in the control room, in the conning tower. Men waited for the explosions that would tell them they had disposed of the hideous menace that had depth-charged them so mercilessly.

'That was the same bugger! I'll swear it on Ned Kelly's grave!'

'Probably, sir. Jerry can't have sent many U-boats out this far.'

H.M.A.S. *Ulmurra* laboured through the russet sea as the sun sank. Look-outs scanned that glittering sea for any sight or sign of the conning tower or periscope of the sub.

'We're short of depth-charges, sir. Only ten left.'

'If we can pick her up again we'll use 'em all up.'

Lieutenant William Blakey stuck his aggressive chin at the Sub.

'Once the tanker gets her fool self lost in the darkness she should be all right and we can go home. But that damned U-boat . . .' Mad Bill Blakey was distinctly unhappy. They had listened for the sub and run in and dropped their stonk and still there had not been the slightest sign that their attacks had had the slightest effect on the Jerry. As Marriott had said, again, wistfully, if only they'd had asdic.

The redness of the sea drew in, as though a bottle of spilled red ink was being righted and the ink sucked back, and the sky shot through with pinks and russets darkened to bruised plum. The Yeoman of Signals kept the look-outs very much on their toes. If the dratted U-boat out there, somewhere under their feet, had not been destroyed or even badly shaken by the stonk, then they could be a target at any minute.

Huge volumes of black smoke belched from *Ul-*

murra's stack. She shuddered and groaned and laboured through the sea. The Chief was doing miracles, but for all those miracles the minesweeping sloop had just not had the turn of speed that would have brought her over the U-boat quickly enough to make sure the depth-charges did their work.

Some time had elapsed since the last attack.

'Nothing yet?' demanded Blakey, fretfully.

'Nothing, sir,' sang out the hydrophone leading seaman.

He was Charley Eastham, and he'd spent his pre-war days singing in a choir on Sundays and working in a Sydney office on weekdays. His musical ear, it was thought, could best be employed listening for U-boats.

'Stop engines,' said Blakey. 'We'll give Charley a chance.'

Ulmurra slowed but continued to surge forward as the light died. Charley Eastham bent in deep concentration. His sensitive fingers turned the dial, swinging the hydrophones in long sweeps. He could hear nothing. On days of good hearing you could hear a submariner stubbing his toe on a watertight door sill and swearing.

'Nothing, sir.'

'Half ahead both.'

The telegraphs rang.

Blakey stared over the canvas dodger and felt like cussing fit to bust.

'Starboard ten.'

'Starboard ten. Ten of starboard wheel on.'

Ulmurra curved through that darkling sea. Each wave top glistered bronze. The sun dropped as though on skates.

'Goddammit to hell!' blazed Blakey. 'Where is that bloody U-boat?'

The sun sank.

In that instant, as though leading the applause at the final curtain, the starboard lookout screamed:

'Torpedoes! Torpedoes running, broad on the starboard beam!'

'Full ahead both. Hard right rudder.'

Blakey gripped the bridge rail and stared over the sea.

Now was the moment for calm. He had steered into the torpedoes' tracks. To have turned away would have taken too long. The stern of *Ulmurra* kicked and began to swing to port. Her bows came around. Blakey felt Marriott at his side. Both men stared out. They could see the torpedoes now, three long streaks of greyish white beneath the shadowed water. In moments they would be gone. Another few minutes and they might never have been spotted at all.

'She's turning,' breathed Marriott.

'Come on, come on, you old cow!' said Blakey. But he spoke calmly, almost as though he was reading the service during church parade on Sunday morning divisions.

Ulmurra swung. The torpedoes passed down her old flanks, two to starboard, one to port, rolling away from her in the wash of her passage.

'Wheel amidships.'

The sloop righted herself from that crazy leaning swing.

'Can you see the bastard, Sub?'

'Nothing ahead, sir. Nothing I can see.'

'He's gone deep. Or else he's still on the surface waiting for us to stop and blow ourselves up on his other kipper. He fired three.'

'Yes, sir.'

The sloop ran on. They could see no sign of periscope, no conning tower, no betraying wash in the shadowed night.

Nothing.

'Bring her onto one-eight-oh.' Blakey walked back to the binnacle. 'We'll run south for five minutes and then turn north again. It might fox him.'

But, an hour later, Mad Bill Blakey had to concede that he was not going to find his U-boat and sink her.

The tussle had been a struggle of wits and will-power, and if Blakey had failed to sink the U-boat, the German had in his turn failed to sink the tanker.

'Call it a draw, sir,' said Marriott.

'Draws are no damn good in this war, Sub. We ought to have sunk the bastard. We had him loud and clear. And then we lost him.'

'A clever skipper down there. Next time—'

'Next time will be when he's sunk thousands of tons of our shipping.'

There was nothing Roger Cruellen-Marriott could say to that, nothing in all decency to mask the feelings he shared with Lieutenant Blakey. They had been offered the chance of a U-boat and they had lost her. They could blame their antiquated ship, their lack of asdic, their shortage of depth-charges. But, when it came down to basics, they both knew they had been up against a master tactician and a damned clever fellow down there in that U-boat.

Befehlshaber des Unterseeboote sent the order for U-42 to return home. She was to make her way north about the British Isles, avoiding the nets and mine-fields of the Channel, and to sink tonnages all the way back to Germany. The High Command of the U-boats had fresh fish to fry in the coming months of 1940.

'The patrol has been a long one,' said Gustav Ludecke, letting his almighty laugh roar out. The sun shone on his white cap as he stood on the bridge. He looked better than he had done immediately after his recovery of consciousness; but to Wolz, standing watch, Daddy looked queasy, greenish of face, with deep haunted eyes encircled by dark rings which gave him a ghostly look.

'We'll use the rest of our eels,' went on Ludecke. 'They'll work. They'll have to work.'

No one could adequately explain how they had missed the British destroyer. They all blamed the torpedoes. They must have malfunctioned. Wolz, although he had not been looking through the attack periscope at the moment of loosing the torpedoes, could hardly think the Commander had missed. The shot had gone nicely with the director angles coming down regularly. The eels must have failed again.

'Seventeen thousand,' said Willi with some disgust.

'Better than some, and better than it might have been.' Wolz was just as much obsessed by tonnage figures as any other U-boat man. Admiral Donitz had said it, it was true, and would remain true. The way to win this war at sea was to sink more and more British ships. Tonnages counted. 'All the same,' he added. 'It's still not good enough. Fifty thousand. That's the target.'

The atmosphere in the boat became more bearable as she sailed northwards. The stifling heat, which gave the men headaches and dizzy spells, eased off. A cooling breeze was once more felt on the bridge. The stores were lasting well, although the bread was more mouldy than not. The sausages continued to be appetizing and the lemonade had not run out. They should make Germany without too much hardship to the stomach. None of this would have been possible without *Rugen*.

As to the atmosphere in the other sense, the mood of the boat, that remained stilted, artificial, worrying to Baldur Wolz. Ludecke was not, in his opinion, in his right mind. Yet it was difficult to put a precise finger on any one thing the Commander did to mark him out – except his intolerable habit of mocking the Nazis and taking every opportunity to poke sly fun at the Fuhrer. This was a common practice among the independent-minded of the Navy; it worried Wolz deeply.

'A corporal,' Ludecke would say. 'I'd very much like

to have an army corporal here now to take a look at the magnetic pistols of the eels. Or strip their gyros down and reassemble.'

Or: 'A brown shirt's a funny colour for a sailor, don't you think, Willi?'

Had Meisten still been alive the report he would have made could have damned Ludecke. And yet Wolz could not bring himself to protest. He was held in the iron discipline of the Navy. And no harm was done. It reminded him of the arguments he'd had with Karl Schramm when Karl and he had gone chasing girls when Rudi had been away from Academy, sick in hospital.

In some low dive, where had they been discovered by the shore patrol they'd have had pyrotechnic rockets fired about their ears by the Captain, they sat and drank beer and watched the girls.

'That dark-eyed one over there,' Karl said, leering. 'The one with the big breasts and the legs – well you don't have to look at her legs.'

'She's not,' said Wolz with the assurance of the very young with limited experience, 'as pretty as the blonde.'

'The great Nordic Blonde,' said Karl, almost sneering, turning on his elbow to stare at Wolz, who wiped suds away and wondered what had got into Karl Schramm. 'The great mother goddess, the myth figure, all bonny, red cheeks, yellow hair and millions of kids.'

'Well—'

'The dark-haired ones. They're the ones with fire. That girl'd wrap her legs around you and squeeze you to death.'

Wolz drank more beer to hide his face. He was, in truth, very young, and resented that. But all the same . . .

Then Karl said something that made Wolz choke.

'She's ripe, all right. Longing for it.' Then: 'She's a Jewess, you know.'

135

'What!' Wolz put his beer down and took out his handkerchief. 'How do you know? She can't be, not here.'

'They all have to live, don't they? Anyway, you can always tell.'

'But – you know about the Jews. We ought to leave.'

'The Block Fuhrer isn't around, Baldur. Anyway, I want her and I've got the cash and so I will. That's one thing they're good for.'

Whether or not Karl had had the girl, Wolz didn't know.

A gang of brownshirts had broken in then and smashed the place up. They'd enjoyed it. Wolz got out amid the din of smashing glass and screaming women and cursing men, ran all the way back. He was panting as he ran. It wasn't the run that made him gasp for breath. The idea that Karl was fool enough to think even for a heartbeat of a Jewess appalled him. Didn't he read the papers? Didn't he listen to the broadcasts? Didn't what the Fuhrer said mean anything to him? Was he so big a fool?

Later when Wolz asked, Karl just shrugged.

'The Nazis do things, Baldur, you wouldn't believe if I told you—'

'Of course there are unpleasant things. I know that. But we have to pull ourselves up by our own efforts. The Fuhrer says—'

Then Karl Schramm made some very objectionable remarks about Adolf Hitler. Wolz was forced to butt in, white with anger.

'Our country was smashed by the Allies! We starved. Our girls starved and died. We were treated with contempt. The Fuhrer has given us back our self-respect! Even you can see that, Karl, for all your high-handed nasty talk.'

'Yes. We have an army and the Luftwaffe and now we're in the Navy. But—'

'No buts, Karl! I'm a good German and the Fuhrer

himself has given our country back its soul—'

'Look around you, Baldur, and think some time.'

When Rudi returned, brimming with news, there remained only two weeks before Karl Schramm was dismissed the class, sent packing from the Academy. Nothing was said. A whisper circulated that his mother was a Jewess, but no one believed that.

So, as Baldur Wolz pondered the problem of his Commander in U-42, he was forced to think of the wild and foolish words of Karl Schramm, and of what might happen to Ludecke if the Commander went on talking in the way he was doing now.

He always held in his mind the words of one of his tutors, Professor Heimrich, who had said with that birdlike nodding of the head: 'The Communists are a blot upon the face of civilization, gentlemen, and one day they will have to be exterminated as one would exterminate vermin. But in one thing they know a truth, for the arch-criminal Lenin has said that you cannot make an omelette without breaking eggs. This is true. Here in Greater Germany we are forging a civilisation that will last a thousand years, and to do that subversive elements must be eliminated, like vermin. True Germany must steel herself. We, gentlemen, must look to the purer future when all the hidden evil-doers have been purged. In that day, our present struggles will be seen in their true light.'

So Karl Schramm had gone, and Wolz had gone to sea, and now, here he was, and his head ached and he just did not know what to do about his Commander.

Such problems had never been envisaged at the Academy. He wanted to sink enemy ships. He did not want to spy on Daddy and perhaps have someone like Cousin Helmut question him . . .

There'd been that cadet over in Bismarck Division they'd found one morning swinging from a coat-hanger by his braces. His tongue had been almost bitten in two. The whispers had hinted darkly at subversive activities, but no-one really knew why he'd killed himself. Rudi, bold and careless, had even hinted that the poor chap hadn't suicided. Maybe, Rudi had said in his offhand, elegant, arisocratic way, maybe he'd been executed for heinous unmentionable crimes against the State.

No one knew. But all felt it could be possible, especially if the chap had been a secret Communist. At least, it saved money that way . . .

The next day they found and destroyed by gunfire a freighter of some seven thousand tons. Two days later they sank a cargo ship of five thousand tons.

Willi rubbed his hands together.

'Now it's beginning to look up, Baldur! That's almost thirty thousand tons. At last we're operating—'

'We've a long way to go, Willi.' Wolz's tone made Willi glance at him sharply. *Rugen*'s midshipman sat slumped in a corner of the wardroom, having not been trusted to stand a watch, and Ludecke spread the watches by taking a trick himself. That, alone, worried Wolz.

Then Willi laughed. 'Oh, you mean we've a long way to reach home. Well, all the better! Plenty of opportunities.'

'Yes, Willi. Of course.'

But Wolz let the calculations flow around in his mind. From the German North Sea ports the distance to mid-Atlantic was two thousand miles, so that meant a four thousand mile round trip before you'd even started. *Rugen* had given U-42 the oil and provisions. The boat would make it back to Germany, if she was not sunk by the English. Once they left the main shipping lanes the pickings would become thin. The British convoys shepherded all the cargo ships along like a herd of sheep. Wolz's ideas on attacking convoys owed a great deal to Donitz's theories as expressed in his book. There, Baldur Wolz was convinced, lay the key to victory in the sea war.

Donitz's doctrine of night attack on the surface made sense. At least, it avoided the horror of depth-charging. This patrol of U-42's was in a very real sense a side-trip, a venture, out of the usual run of submarine warfare as envisaged. U-42 had been detailed to cause dislocation on distant trade routes and by her mere presence cause confusion and grief to the enemy. These laudable aims she had accomplished. In addition, in the fate of *Rugen*, U-42 had also demonstrated the advantages of a submarine raider over a surface raider, for all the romance of the latter. Great Britain would be forced to expend a vast amount of effort and treasure in combating the menace of the U-boats, and the farther afield these efforts could be spread the better.

Sparks began to fly from the radio room.

Ludecke called his officers together. He held a signal form in his hand. Wolz felt a stab of concern at the gaunt, skull-like look of the skipper. Ludecke was living on his nerves and the effort it was costing him showed.

The Commander opened his remarks by saying, bluntly, that U-42 could not live through another severe depth-charge attack.

Wolz did not feel called upon to answer.

Willi said: 'It was rough, yes, I agree. But the old boat will bring us through—'

'You just don't understand, Willi!' Ludecke spoke with temper. He appeared to be holding himself in with tremendous strain. The lines were grooved deeply into his skin, which had a curious pebbly look.

'But—' said Willi.

The Commander waved the signal. 'BdU orders us to attack a most important target on our way. U-40 also.' He did not mention the name of the target. He did not appear, really, to be fully aware of what he was doing. That damned .303! It had cost this man more than a simple wound, and Wolz cursed his own helplessness. He had never in his worst imaginings ever anticipated he would be forced to witness Ludecke in this state.

The signal form shook in Ludecke's grasping fingers.

Wolz cleared his throat. 'What is the target? Perhaps—'

'There's no perhaps about it. You'll have to take the wagtail up, Herr Leutnant. You can put your gift for command to some use in the air. Spot for us. We should be running onto the target within a couple of hours – if those dry-land sailors have done their sums right.'

Wolz could not look at Willi.

Then Ludecke added: 'After that I shall decide if we attack, or not.'

'Do we have any latitude in our orders?' began Wolz.

Ludecke flared up. Muscles jumped along his jaws, and his pale eyes held a glaring, blank look that filled Wolz with the fear of madness.

'I am in command, Herr Leutnant, a fact you would do well not to forget. I have not forgotten. If there are destroyers in force – well, let us wait and see.'

Wolz persisted. He made himself say the words.

'But we will meet destroyers anyway. We have to attack if those are our orders. The English must put out destroyers in a screen and we must penetrate and attack. If we allow the mere presence of destroyers to deter us, then—'

Ludecke did not strike him. He turned those pale and staring eyes upon his second-in-command and looked through him.

'Take the Bachstelze up, Herr Leutnant, and spot for us. I shall tell you what to do when the time comes.'

All that Wolz could say was: 'Very good!'

The gyro-kite was brought out and assembled and Wolz donned flying gear. The air still held the warmth of more southerly regions, but it would be nippy enough aloft to kit up fully. The breeze blew freshly enough for easy flying conditions. A few bundles of clouds drifted; otherwise the sky arched blue and semi-transparent, as though you could reach up your hand right through that gossamer sheen and pluck whatever fate held in store for you from the deepest recesses of the universe.

Mildly amused at his flight of fancy Wolz watched as the men assembled the kite, occasionally letting go a pungent comment on five-thumbed so-called mechanics. The hands from *Rugen* were happy enough to assist; poor devils, they'd had a really rough time of it. The midshipman was still not fully recovered from the effects of the depth-charging. His screams in retrospect still had power to make Wolz not only angry but embarrassed.

If a fellow capitulated to fear like that he had no place in the Kriegsmarine, and certainly, most certainly, no place whatsoever in a U-boat.

Ludecke looked on from the bridge, his white cap at a slant over the bandage, his eyes black pits, smudges above the sunken cheeks over which the harsh stubble had now grown into a beard. They were all a dishevelled lot. No one wore a proper uniform. Smart uniforms, all tiddly, were for leave at home. They looked, Wolz considered with some satisfaction as he strapped in, just like a gang of cut-throat pirates.

Up span the Bachstelze, the rotors spinning whorls of light, up and up, tethered by her umbilical cord. Wolz swung her gently this way and that. Again he luxuriated in the marvellous sense of flying, and damned the restraining wire.

The horizon stretched around him, a blank circle misty and indistinct, making him realise afresh just how damn big the world was. Water ran and surged everywhere about him, and below, as though being towed along by his kite, the slim metal cigar of the U-boat looked tiny, toy-like, frail and fragile, lost in the immensity of ocean.

The colours enchanted Wolz. Subtle distinctions in the blue and grey of the sea and sky, the green tinge of the Atlantic, the mother-of-pearl lincrusta edges to the clouds, the long slanting rays of the sun striking the sea in constantly changing splinters of gold. The Zeiss in his hands swung and steadied. He looked carefully.

He spoke into the phone unemotionally, as befitted a U-boat officer of the German Navy in sight of wonderful prey.

'Ship bearing three-two-oh, range thirty-five thousand.' A cloud fluffed past obscuring his vision. But he had seen enough – enough, at least, to convince a man who had spent hour after hour studying and memorising the silhouettes of enemy warships. 'Aircraft carrier.'

Ludecke's excited yell bounced up the wire.

'Aircraft carrier! You're sure, Baldur?'

'Positive. I would say she is *Ark Royal*.'

Ludecke laughed. The laugh sounded genuine and spontaneous, making Wolz feel a sudden warmth for the skipper, making him hope Daddy was back on form, his wound forgotten.

'*Ark Royal*? Now, now, Baldur, you know that is impossible. Why, didn't Goering personally assure us that the famous *Ark Royal* had been sent to the bottom? Didn't that Stuka pilot, now Herr Leutnant Adolph Francke, sink her with a single bomb? Goebbels has said so, you know, Baldur.' Ludecke's words puzzled Wolz. Before he could speak again, Ludecke went on: 'She can't be *Courageous*, of course, for Otto Schuhart got her in U-29. So, if she really is a carrier, she must be *Glorious* – unless your eyes deceive you and she's smaller than you think, *Hermes*, for example.'

The cloud passed, thinning to leave a few isolated wisps. Conscientiously Wolz held the Zeiss level and steady and drew a breath and held it and stared intently at that long tall grey shape. She was a long way off. But he was certain. He picked out salient details, and was sure.

'*Ark Royal*.'

Ludecke drew a breath, clearly audible over the wire.

'BdU said a carrier; she's been harassing our supply ships. She was off the Plate, too, helping to destroy *Graf Spee*, or so I understand. But *Ark Royal*—' Then, in a sharp, cutting tone: 'Destroyers?'

'At least four.'

Wolz knew that the distant look-outs could not see him floating in the air in his water wagtail. At least, he had that advantage. But, having given the Commander the course, speed and range of the target, whoever she might be, they must now be after her, sharpish.

A few more wisps of cloud obscured the sight. But Wolz had seen enough.

'I'd better be winched down and we can—'' he began.

Ludecke's voice contained that new and painful intolerant viciousness.

'I'll do the thinking and give the orders, Herr Leutnant! If she is a carrier and not a tanker – take very great care—' And, then, again in that puzzling, almost bantering tone: 'After all, when the Herr Reichmarschall Goering is kind enough to inform us that his Stukas have taken care of *Ark Royal* so we no longer have to worry about her – after all, Herr Leutnant, in view of that how can you continue to maintain that you can see a ship that has sunk beneath the waves?'

The sarcasm struck home forcibly to Wolz. He felt the pain of Ludecke's condition. But he knew the British fleet. He knew every damn ship in that mighty concourse and he was not one to make a mistake about things of that nature.

'*Ark Royal*,' he said again, stubbornly.

His attention had been concentrated upon that distant and menacing shape. The grey bulk slid beyond concealing cloud. The Bachstelze gave a shudder and a swing to starboard and almost unthinkingly Wolz brought her back onto an even keel, aligned with U-42 on the end of the wire.

He swung his Zeiss about the horizon, methodically sweeping through west and south and so on to southeast where a mass of cloud piled up thunderheads, white and grey and glistening high into the sky.

A black dot darted between two piled masses.

Wolz stared hard, feeling his heart kicking, feeling the abrupt dryness in his throat.

'Aircraft! Bearing one-four-oh! Flying straight for us!'

No time to winch in now.

Feeling as though he struggled in nightmare against restricting bands Wolz pulled the lever to jettison the rotors. The tubular fuselage frame fell away and he kicked free. The parachute opened as he fell, opened sufficiently to break his fall – in theory.

He hoped. He felt the wind bristling past his plunging body. The fuselage hit the sea in a spreading white spray.

More white spray fumed up.

U-42 was flooding!

He saw the vents spouting water, saw the conning tower sliding under, saw the stern lifting. White water spilled away from her stern as her screws span.

'No!' screamed Baldur Wolz. 'No!'

But U-42 slid beneath the waters of the Atlantic.

The chute caught and held him.

He swayed for a few moments and then his booted feet hit the water and he was gasping and choking with the canopy half over him, holding him down.

With a convulsive effort he broke free, spitting water, struggling up. A turn of the lock on his stomach and a savage blow with his fist freed the harness.

The chute drifted, turning and ribboning.

He looked up.

The aeroplane was passing overhead.

He saw her.

She was a Swordfish, what his English friends called a Stringbag, and the reason for that was quite clear.

She flew on, level and serene. Her engine sputtered evenly. The sun shafted a watery gleam from her wings. Her propeller span in a disc of light. Then she was gone, roaring away to the horizon and her parent ship.

Baldur Wolz floated, alone and friendless, on the hostile sea.

CHAPTER TWELVE

After a time the idea that he was going to die made Baldur Wolz's headache clear up quite miraculously.

Everybody had to die. It was a cliché of living. He lay back on his horseshoe-shaped lifebelt and decided that he might as well savour what dying was like. Living had been fun. Or, at least, a lot of it. Some had been hell, of course.

Water slopped across his face and he spat, but he did not rub his eyes.

Yes, in his relatively short life he'd crammed in quite a few experiences. And he'd never regret deciding to be a U-boat man. He wished he could have known his father. He gave a passing curse to the stupid oafs in the minesweeper which had run his father's boat down, just as the war was finishing. His father would have been proud to have scuttled his boat as the Fleet had been scuttled in Scapa Flow. That was one in the eye for the English all right.

He could see only sea and sky and clouds. His own body looked misshapen, floating in the water, the flying gear keeping him reasonably warm. He'd die soon, anyway, and then he needn't worry any more.

Those idiots in the Swordfish! Mind you, Wolz rather fancied he'd made a serious mistake. He should have been maintaining a proper watch all the time, taking checking observations of the carrier. It was obvious that she'd be flying off aircraft and the chances of one crossing U-42's track was always on.

Yes, he should have spotted the Stringbag before he did.

But, as for the Tommies flying her! Blind! Blind, completely sightless. How could they have missed a U-boat diving? And they'd not seen either him or his parachute – but then, he was a remarkably small object in a sea feathered with spitting whitecaps. To spot a man in the sea was a job of the utmost difficulty, calling for quantities of luck that, he suspected, had run out for him.

No doubt the Tommies in the Swordfish with *Ark Royal* in sight had their minds fixed on tea and biscuits.

And, despite that poor devil Ludecke, she was *Ark Royal*. She *was*. The Luftwaffe had bungled again.

His mind drifted as he drifted.

Sweet little Lottie, so moist and warm and inviting . . .

They'd romped in fine style, the pair of them, all over the schloss, in the bedrooms, in the kitchens and the still-room, in the pantry, up the stairs, each flight taken as a separate place to romp afresh. Lottie, giggling, her nightdress all askew, had taken infinite delight in dreaming up fresh places to explore and conquer and permanently mark as their own.

They'd crawled up to the attic among the dust and cobwebs and Lottie had sprawled out with her white nightdress all a ghostly shimmer in the moonlight through the circular windows, and he'd felt his lust rising all over again. She had a way with her, had Lottie, and she'd suck him dry – so she said with her high, little-girl laugh that, besides infuriating him with its inanity, goaded him to sexual feats that left him gasping like a stranded fish.

The second time the family had paid a call on their neighbour, the Baroness von Hartstein and her daughter Trudi, Wolz had been feeling like a puppy-dog shaken in the jaws of a tiger, limp as a dishrag. His eyelids were puffy and heavy. His head ached. And yet he was waiting with a feverish impatience for the night, when Lottie and he would seek to stake out fresh conquests in the maze of ancient rooms and corridors.

The first visit they'd paid Baroness Elizabeth had

147

been merely a formal one, most punctilious, highly-polished boots clicking and much bowing over white extended hands.

This time Cousin Manfred, immaculate in his Luft-waffe uniform went, as he told Wolz, with more urgent designs. They'd strolled in the grounds of the castle whilst the Baroness and Uncle Siegfried talked slowly and with courtesy in the Emerald drawing room with its peacock fans and lustrous furniture and garnitures of armour around the walls. Because Cousin Siegfried, as dapper and immaculate as his brother in his SS uniform, accompanied them, Wolz felt he could go along as well. Cousin Manfred was not pleased. But Cousin Siegfried, his black breeches marvels of flaring precision over the mirrors of his black boots, laughed and insisted, so the four young people strolled among the flower beds.

Wolz, because it was the custom, wore civilian clothes.

Cousin Siegfried made a tiny, almost contemptuous, gesture.

'You'll have to wear uniform all the time, soon, Baldur.'

'Time enough for that.'

Manfred drew Wolz aside, whispering.

'Get Siegfried off my back, Baldur, for pity's sake! I'm so hot for Trudi I don't know what I'll do.'

Wolz smiled. 'If I do you will, and if I don't, you won't. Maybe it would be safer if I didn't.'

'You're just a damned traitor to an old friend!'

'Suppose Siegfried won't be drawn? I think he fancies the luscious Trudi himself.'

'I'll pulverise him! She's mine!'

Looking at the elegant black-clad form of the SS man and the slender, laughing girl, Wolz wondered if he ought, in all conscience, to allow either of them, Luftwaffe or S.S. to best the Navy in so important a matter. It was a matter of honour ...

There was no doubt at all that Trudi was a morsel. She had that pale-faced and yet alive quality of good looks one associated with German maidens, floating down the Rhine on the white backs of swans ... It was all romantic nonsense and he wondered with some warmth how she performed in bed. She was built for amatory combat, with a small waist and breasts that, in the fashionable long-line jersey, thrust alluringly. The length of her thigh, too, indicated strength. Her hips were, perhaps, a little on the broad side. But that was a vitally important matter in the breeding of good German children, and Wolz was well aware of the value of comfort over speed in that area.

So, on the pretext of discussing the role of the S.S. in the Army – or, as he very quickly corrected himself – of the S.S. as a powerful military force alongside the Army, a force, as Siegfried, at once engaged confirmed with enthusiasm, that would teach the tradition-bound Army a few tricks, Wolz was able to draw the S.S. man away past a bed of roses that had bloomed most gloriously and were now cut back ready for the winter.

The last he saw of Manfred, the Luftwaffe fighter pilot had ventured an arm about the luscious waist, his head thrown back, the blond hair very brave, laughing, leading Trudi along a leaf-strewn path. Wolz wished him luck. He would himself essay the charmed castle at the first opportunity, which was likely to be some way off, given the future before him.

'But the Navy,' Siegfried was saying, apparently with some connection to S.S. affairs. 'You are all aloof, out of the main stream. Even Manfred, for all his posing, is in the Luftwaffe and therefore is exercising a real pressure on events.'

Wolz refused to allow himself to become annoyed.

In a way that many people had thought strange he had always liked his three cousins and got on well with them. As for Lisl, he put her out of his mind and concentrated on what Siegfried was saying, and the memory of the way Trudi had walked, very swayingly, as Manfred led her off. Yes, he'd got on very well with Siegfried, Manfred and Helmut. That was almost contrary to nature, and certainly contrary to fiction. Now, of course, Helmut had changed, become cold and grim and distant; but he was always courteous to Baldur Wolz and, Wolz felt sure, underneath his icy determinism the old friendship persisted. As for Siegfried, his enthusiasm for the S.S. and for the new Germany could not fail to be infectious. He so obviously believed he was a member of the master race – as he was, of course – that Wolz could still catch much of that old comradeship.

'You should have joined the S.S., Baldur. We are going to order the way the world runs.'

'And you mean the Navy will have no part?'

'No – at least, not for me. I don't forget the times we have had – and you were always the best swimmer! But Germany is a land empire and we must look east—'

'We will have to make the English see that first.'

'The English. They are decadent – we all know that, even if not as bad as the French – but they will see reason. They must. All they need is a little discipline to tighten them up. My S.S. will do a power of good to the English, in due time.'

'Yes, that may be true. But, now, we in the Navy must fight them. And we in the U-boat service are doing the fighting.'

Cousin Siegfried digested that.

Then he said with some acerbity: 'All credence in the British Navy has been lost since the Skagerrak. They were decisively beaten. Even the Americans say so.'

'Jutland,' said Wolz. 'The naval doctrine says we won. But you and I both know, my dear Siegfried, that it is an odd victory that sees the defeated in possession of the field and waiting for the victorious to show their noses again.'

'You spent too much time in England.' Siegfried punched him lightly on the shoulder. In the old days that would have led to a laughing scuffling tussle. Now Wolz smiled.

'Oh, I don't deny I can see things from an English point of view, and I think that is valuable. Know your enemy, you know, and all that.'

'So long as you do not become tainted with his philosophy.'

'Philosophy?' said Wolz. 'And the English?' He laughed. 'They run a mile if you mention the word. It's all horses and beer and football and if you mention Kant or Hegel or Descartes they think they're running in the two-thirty at Ascot and enquire the starting prices.'

Siegfried laughed, also, and the two men walked amicably along the gravel path, still arguing. Wolz knew that the old German Navy had had better ships and better gunnery than the English in the great sea-battle of 1916; but all the same he knew, sombrely and with a chill, that the English supremacy on the seas and seaways had not been broken, only a little deflected, and the Royal Navy remained a most potent instrument of war. It was up to Donitz and the U-boats to change that ...

Trudi appeared around the corner, past the evergreens. She was walking rapidly. She was smoothing down her jersey dress. Two roses bloomed in her cheeks. Her breasts rose and fell rapidly. When she saw the two, the S.S. officer and the Naval leutnant in civilian clothes, she slowed her rapid walk. She smiled brilliantly.

'Hullo, you two! Deciding the fate of the world between you?'

She danced up to them, parting them and swung around. She put her arms through theirs and so walked along between them, one on each arm, in a manner that would have scandalised an older generation.

'I see the Stukas have been dive-bombing again,' remarked Siegfried, addressing the evergreens.

'Or the 109s have been strafing,' said Wolz. He could not stop himself from laughing. This Trudi was a brilliant girl, with a lush shape, and a fire in her for all her pale golden pallidness, giving the lie to poor Karl Schramm and his theories about dark girls. Perhaps old Manfred had thrust his throttle too far forward and gone screaming down with his engine revving past the boost mark. That was just like him.

In a minute or two they saw the Luftwaffe uniform proceeding very smartly across the lawn towards the conservatory. Trudi eyed the disappearing Manfred.

'The Luftwaffe spearheaded the Blitzkreig,' she said, sparkling with malicious amusement. 'I think it up to the S.S. and the Navy to take their share.'

Siegfried looked across her golden hair at Wolz. Wolz said: 'I agree. I think I will see what Manfred has to say.'

As he walked off, he thought to himself that he was not being a fool. He'd been fair to Siegfried. Now it was his turn. But Wolz had not failed to observe the way Trudi's hip had thrust against him as she walked, a deliberate and provocative action, tantalising him. If she was rubbing her hip against him then she wouldn't be doing the same for Siegfried. Not even in the way she walked, with everything swaying from starboard to port, and back to starboard again.

Whatever luck Siegfried had, he was not in a happy mood when they left for the drive back to the schloss.

That night they were to entertain the fetching Marlene again. Siegfried growled at Manfred when the Luftwaffe pilot enquired, not too politely, how he had fared.

Wolz sat back – for Manfred drove – and smiled to himself and reflected that the observer saw most of the game, and the cat who waited got the cream.

The delectable Trudi would keep.

Tonight they would revel with the S.S. and Party officials in the blatant sexuality of Marlene.

She appeared again, clad even more outrageously in her S.S. straps and Walther pistol and polished black boots. The S.S. cap and the skull emblem and all the rest of it, the red and black gaudy against her naked body, gave Wolz the trembling feeling of new ages opening, ages in which anything might be possible.

Marlene sang and danced and flaunted herself and the gathered officers sang and got drunk and were sick and sorted themselves out partners. Wolz took himself off to the garage and drove quietly and carefully back to the Hartstein castle, so much older and grander than his uncle's place, and yet run down and unkempt, with the lack of money making maintenance desperately difficult.

He admitted to himself that he was not altogether sure of what he was doing. She would think it most odd for a young man to call so late at night, a young man, moreover, whom she had only just met and who must smell somewhat strongly of schnapps. All the same, he was determined to see her.

He was let into the draughty old hall by a manservant with a branched candlestick who blinked owlishly at him.

'The Fraulein Trudi? She is asleep. The Baroness—'

'Let the Baroness sleep on. It is Fraulein Trudi whom I wish to see.'

The manservant, a bent and grumbling figure in nightshirt and nightcap and slopping slippers, at last brought Trudi. She wore a long midnight-blue dressing gown, gathered about her neck by one slender hand, her hair unbraided and falling about her shoulders. The shadows of the hall lay long and eerie across the floor, among the voluminous drapes and the massive furniture. The manservant took himself off and the two were left in the faint radiance of a candlestick on the black oak sideboard. Portraits frowned down. Trudi stared at him, her eyebrows raised.

'This is very late, Herr Leutnant, to call—'

Wolz had no idea what to say, what excuse to give.

He stammered. 'I thought—' She looked marvellous. Then inspiration came. 'I have to report – and I did not say goodbye.'

Her quick response touched him.

She came two steps down the stairs, her hand trailing on the balustrade.

'You are going to sea?'

He scraped up a laugh from the bilges.

'There might be an English spy under the window seat – Trudi. I cannot tell you where I'm going. But I wanted to say goodbye.'

'I understand.'

She came down two more steps. The candlelight shone in her hair. Her lips were half-parted, moist and sweet. Wolz took two steps up. Now they stood, on a level. She put out her hand, letting go the balustrade, as though abandoning a sure anchorage and casting herself onto whatever the seas of fate might bring.

Wolz bent, put his arms about her. He kissed her very gently. Yet he put a great deal into the kiss. She responded. Her arms lifted and the robe fell away. He saw a white nightdress, lace, the curved swell of breasts – strange how their curves always reminded him – and then she pushed him away and he caught his heel on the staircarpet, twisted, and fell.

At once she was at his side.

'Oh, Baldur! I did not mean to – you are not hurt?'

He let out a whooshing breath. The floor was damned hard.

'No, Trudi. It'd take more than that to scupper me.'

She knelt at his side. He looked at her. Her face bent

over his, concerned, her eyes wide. Her hair flowed over her cheeks. He put up a hand, and touched her cheek and she did not pull away.

'Baldur—'

'Hush. Hush.'

He sat up and put his arm over her shoulders and pulled her down. He could feel her warmth against him. She made all the flaunting nudity of Marlene seem the trash it was.

He pulled her towards him with his left arm and his right hand pressed her waist. She opened her lips. He could see the ripeness and the moistness. He shifted his right hand, feeling the flimsy material of the nightdress rumpling and sliding. Her skin felt cool, cool and smooth. His hand cupped her breast. It lay in his hand, heavy and round and smooth.

He pulled her down to kiss her again and with a cry, a sob he thought almost despairing, she pulled away, stood up.

She was panting. The blood stained her face. The candlelight threw her body into bold light and shadows.

'Baldur! I cannot. You should not— Please go.'

He stood up slowly and automatically brushed his clothes, straightening his twisted jacket. His white shirt glimmered in the candlelight. He put out a hand. But she drew back.

'Please go, Baldur.'

'When I am home on leave again. I shall see you?'

She regarded him levelly, serious, her eyes catching the candlelight. She moistened her lips.

'Yes. Yes, I think so.' She whispered the words, and she did not look at him.

So he took himself off. He was not altogether dispirited. It had been a foolish thing to do and no doubt Trudi was going to have to do some fast explaining to her mother the Baroness. But, at the least, Baldur

Wolz felt he had opened his score and could look forward to a triumph on his return.

A wave slashed him across the face and he coughed and choked. The lifebelt swung him around. He was alone on the hostile sea.

CHAPTER THIRTEEN

He was not dead yet.

But he would be dead soon.

There would be no return to Trudi. Or to Lottie or Heidi. Not even the shadow of a return to Lisl, to whom he had never been close enough to say that he could go away. Aloof, remote, living in her own world, Lisl remained for him unattainable. He could not bear to think of her.

All these women – and here he was drifting in his silly lifebelt in the mid-Atlantic abandoned, dying – or about to die.

It really was too ridiculous.

He could feel the blood in him, the strength of his body, the thoughts tumbling in a hurly-burly through his mind. Why should he have to die and leave the world now?

It was not just ridiculous – it was damned unfair.

He twisted himself around and looked at his watch. To his surprise he'd been in the water a bare fifteen minutes. That astonished him.

He'd looked at his watch by the little flame of his lighter, in the shrubbery, as he'd walked up to the schloss. He'd put the car away very carefully. Lights blazed from many windows and the sounds of revelry carried clearly on the crisp night air. He'd walked in, quietly, not wishing to attract any attention and questions. He stepped over the drunken body of an S.S. man and started for the back stairs.

A girl screamed in the shadows by the oaken door and he'd smiled, thinking someone was having better luck than himself.

Heidi, Lottie's friend, staggered out. Her dress was torn away, dragging around her hips. Her hair swung in a dishevelled mass about her face which was flushed and tear-stained. A trickle of blood ran from a split lip, and there were the beginnings to two or three bruises on her cheeks and jaws.

Wolz stopped and stared in the half light.

An S.S. man lurched out. His uniform hung open; but Wolz could see the collar patches, and the two bars and three stars of a Hauptsturmfuhrer. Siegfried was a Hauptsturmfuhrer and he had confided to Wolz, in his heavy way that so often overrode his old excited enthusiasm, that he would soon be made up to Sturmbannfuhrer. This fellow, now, Wolz had been told, had just been promoted from Obersturmfuhrer and was filled with his own importance.

'Come here, you bitch,' the Captain called, thickly, reaching for Heidi. 'Stop playing coy, you little whore.'

Heidi did not recognise Wolz in the shadows. She saw a shadow and she gasped and held up her arms. She'd have bruises on the soft flesh of the inside of her arms and her biceps, that was clear. The S.S. man lurched on and caught at the white strap of her brassiere.

'You little bitch!'

Wolz stepped forward. He hated himself for getting into a situation like this. But Heidi was as free with her favours as Lottie, and if this drunken boor had to do what, evidently, he had been doing to Heidi to get his pleasure, then Wolz could see with unpleasant clarity that Heidi wanted nothing of it.

'Stand aside, Hauptsturmfuhrer,' said Wolz. He felt the ludicrousness of his words. 'The young lady is obviously not—'

The S.S. man peered, trying to see. 'She's obviously no lady, you cretin. Get out of my way.'

For, somehow, Heidi was behind Wolz, and he was standing straight before the S.S. officer. The fellow made a mistake. With a foul oath he lashed out at Wolz.

His blow could be slipped easily enough. Wolz moved. He tried to catch the man's arm, to quieten him down, to reason with him, and the S.S. kick came in with a full-blooded smash of a black-booted foot.

Wolz felt the kick shatter on his thigh, and he felt the blood go thumping round his body. He couldn't stop himself.

He hit the S.S. man in the guts and doubled him up. There was a deal of venom in the blow. But his adversary was not put down. With a scream of rage he leaped in, lashing out, bashing a series of vicious blows at Wolz. Wolz ducked and parried and then struck back, hard. The Navy taught its people to fight. He hit the S.S. man in the guts, kicked him in the groin, smashed him on the back of the head as he went down. He found that he wanted to kick his face in. He was shaking with rage.

Heidi shrank back, voiceless with fear.

The S.S. man groaned and writhed around, trying to rise. He got a grip on Wolz's leg and pulled him down. They scuffled on the floor. A fist hit Wolz in the guts and he grunted. He put his knee on the fellow's windpipe and seized his hair and bashed his head crackingly on the old polished floorboards.

'You bastard!' Bash went the head, the man's eyes snapping open and shut, his mouth gagging. 'You bastard!' Crash went the head against the floor.

Somehow, from somewhere, common sense flooded in. He could have killed the idiot.

He stood up, trembling, breathing in huge dragging draughts of air.

Heidi ran to him and threw her arms about him. Her naked breasts dangled from the broken barrier of the brassiere. Quite unthinkingly, Wolz put his arm about her, filling his hand with flesh. His other hand raked down. Heidi squealed and then melted in to him.

'It is Baldur—?'

'Leave the fool. Let us hope he has the sense to say he fell down the stairs.'

Wolz lifted Heidi. He held her in his arms. He bent and kissed her and she squirmed and he remembered her split lip.

He drew back.

She trembled against him. 'I was frightened. He wanted—'

'He got what he was asking for. Now you and I, Heidi ...'

He carried her upstairs and threw her on his bed and stripped off his jacket. He bundled it away in a wardrobe. Blood stained the lapels. He'd have to have that cleaned. But Heidi lay on the bed, her body shadowed by the lamp, white and demanding, her hair glittering gold. He leaped on her. She squealed, but her squeal bore no relation to her frightened scream as she'd staggered terrified from the S.S. Hauptsturmfuhrer.

'Oh, Baldur—' She held him and he squirmed into a more comfortable position. Her warmth and nearness did not so much dizzy him as inflame him. Even when they lay together quiet and spent he was still thinking of Trudi, and wondering why it had to be poor silly Heidi and not Trudi here with him.

Nothing was said on the following day about the idiot S.S. man, except for Siegfried, offhandedly, saying the man had had to leave early. Wolz, too, was leaving, due to report back to U-42. If any more was to come of it, it must wait until he returned from patrol.

The moving surge beneath him was not the frantic body of Heidi. The water lifted and dropped him. He felt the wetness against his face. Well, if he couldn't have a woman before he died then he'd damn well have a cigar.

That was the thing. Never give in in the face of defeat. Defeat was an old adversary. The Imperial German Navy had been defeated. There was no doubt of that. The English had really won at Jutland, no matter what the naval pundits said. The cost of the victory had been high, but that was because they'd had rotten ships and indifferent gunnery. And that was because their global role demanded long-range ships and not the specially designed ships of the Germans, aimed for the North Sea, and because of a natural defect of the English character which led to over-casualness in preparation. Even so, as the sea washed him up and down and he extracted his slim silver cigar case, even so he knew the Germans had had to realise the power of the Royal Navy over the world in the battle of the Falkland Islands. There long-range ships had proved what they could do.

He put the cigar in his mouth, gripping his teeth down hard. He'd not light it with the spray slashing at him and the water sloshing over him, but he could still chew.

So, chewing on his cigar and thinking pleasant thoughts about parties and drinks and girls, Baldur Wolz waited for the end.

A thin tube showed in the water a hundred metres off.

Wolz stared at it owlishly.

He was still staring, chewing on his cigar, when the water boiled away in a froth-surrounded dome. The water ran and splashed and white-water blew with a loud hissing and a long steel shape rose into view, spilling water. The clang of the hatch sounded unnaturally loud.

Wolz goggled.

The conning tower, still spouting water, rose up and lifted easily through the sea.

A white cap appeared on the bridge.

Galvanised, Wolz lifted an arm.

He took out the cigar and yelled. He waved and yelled like a crazy man. Water ran over his face.

They fished him out with a boathook.

He crawled up onto the casing, and stood up, and his legs felt most peculiar. He found he was still chewing on the cigar. He looked up at the bridge.

The Commander peered over, looking down at him. It was not Gustav Ludecke.

Still feeling as though he was dreaming, Wolz took the cigar from his mouth with his left hand, and sizzled up a salute with his right.

'Beg to report Leutnant zur See Baldur Wolz!'

He jammed the cigar back and started for the bridge ladder.

'Welcome aboard, Herr Leutnant.'

'Otto Kuppisch,' said Wolz, feeling that he was not standing where he was. 'U-40.'

He was back in a U-boat. The sensation smote him strangely. His thoughts had twined around Germany, and the S.S., and cars and parties and drinks. The S.S. were a clanny bunch. He felt mortally unsure about the effects of his fight with the S.S. officer who had been attempting Heidi. That Siegfried was his friend might mean nothing. But, here he was, back with comrades of the Navy about him, the smiling faces, the thick beards, the rakish caps, the old oily scruffy scraps of clothing masquerading as uniforms. The smell of a U-boat, the oil and pitch and seawater and stale cabbage – he felt a tremendous jolt go through him and he swayed.

'U-40,' said Kapitanleutnant Otto Kuppisch. A slender, elegant man with pebbly-grey eyes, a ragged swatch of blond beard about his jaws, a broken nose, he gripped Wolz's elbow, looking concerned. 'You are all right?'

'Yes, thank you. Perfectly.'

Kuppisch smiled. He pushed his white commander's cap back. 'Well, you're a cool customer. We fish you out of the drink and there you are, smoking a cigar in mid-Atlantic.'

'Hardly smoking.'

'No, well, I understand. You'd better get below and dry out. Let our Sanitatsobermaat have a look at you.'

Wolz nodded and went to push past towards the hatch, well knowing that no U-boat commander wanted useless bodies cluttering up his bridge; then he checked.

'*Ark Royal*,' he said, turning abruptly.

Otto Kuppisch was a man who had grasped essentials. He had seen Wolz's flying clothing, the Zeiss still dangling on their straps about his neck. He knew what happened if a boat had to dive in emergency with the water wagtail aloft.

'So that's the target. We have been directed into this area to look for a carrier. BdU did not specify.'

'Perhaps they were tender for the Luftwaffe's feelings.'

'It is possible.' Kuppisch would not allow himself to be drawn on interservice rivalries and similar nonsenses. He ran a tight boat. 'Tell me of your boat, Herr Leutnant.'

'U-42.'

'She is sunk?'

'No – I hope not. I was up – had to take a swim – then you turned up—'

Kuppisch interrupted.

'You have seen *Ark Royal*, or you would not know the name of the carrier. Bearing, range, course?'

His words spat out as they used to spit out commands at Academy when you were in the last stages of exhaustion and still had an hour's torture to last through. Wolz stiffened and gave the course, range and bearing. He added: 'There were four destroyers, also.'

'Destroyers. Well, they are like vermin; they must be lived with and squashed when possible. Now get you below. We have had trouble with Number Five vent, the damn valve's sticking. But the old U-40 will get us there. And we have just one eel left.'

With his head sticking out of the hatch, Wolz looked

163

up, his professional interest aroused.

'You have had trouble with the torpedoes?'

'But yes! Damn eels. We've stripped this last one down to its underpants. It's going to work, this time. I'll tell BdU a few things about their damned eels when we get back, I assure you, Herr Leutnant.'

Clumping down the ladder Wolz felt a warmth that came not just from the close, smelly, oily interior of the boat. Rather, he felt that Kapitanleutnant Otto Kuppisch was a U-boat skipper with whom he could do business.

He had been rescued from the sea, found drifting in the middle of nowhere, and yet the business of being a U-boat man went on uninterrupted, as though the event was one of the most ordinary imaginable. There would be a big party later on, and lots of excited talk and incredulous marvellings; but, now, they were professionals and there was a job to do and the job must be done, despite all obstacles. That was the German way.

U-40 crashed through the sea, her diesels running flat out, spuming up flying sheets of spray. The lookouts kept vigilantly on the alert. Their Zeiss did not leave their eyes. Down in the wardroom Wolz drank hot coffee – and he admitted that the stuff this time tasted heavenly – and pictured the look-outs in the bridge quartering every single part of the horizon as well as the bearing on which they raced towards *Ark Royal*. He thought of poor Speidel, and reflected that a man's chances of death could be weighed by a feather, give or take the machinations of chance.

He must be light-headed. No wonder, really, after his experience. The boat's Number One was on the bridge with the skipper, but the Number Two, a tired-looking fellow with bags under his eyes, rolled out to talk. The Number Three had been lost overside in a gale when his Steinback safety straps had parted, metal reinforcements or no metal reinforcements.

The Sanitatsobermaat came into the wardroom with his bag from which he began to produce a variety of pills and tonics. Wolz did not smile. The chap had a job to do, and intended to do it properly.

'I was only in the water for a half hour or so,' said Wolz. It was a mild protest.

'Take this—' and a pill popped into his mouth. 'Drink this.' He drank. Then: 'You should get some rest, Herr Leutnant. These things can take funny turns.'

'I'll be all right. But, thank you.'

'You're a lucky man to be alive – and that's God's truth.'

The sick-berth attendant was right, no doubt of it.

His wet clothes had been taken away and he was rigged out in a mess of slops, but he felt wonderful. He was still alive. U-40 thrummed through the sea as Otto Kubisch drove her on to achieve a good attacking position according to the information given him by Leutnant Wolz, who had been summed up by Kapitanleutnant Kuppisch as a highly-skilled officer – and cool! Damned cool. Floating abandoned in the sea chewing on a cigar!

Wolz realised how lucky he'd been. That the two U-boats should be in the same square was to be expected, given that Donitz had instructed them to go there. But to have popped up on the same pinpoint, that was the marvel. Wolz was reminded of his feelings at Siegfried's S.S. party, when the revelation of new ages opening before him had struck him so vividly, the idea that the future held all things and all things were possible. Now he felt like a man who had cheated death and for whom, therefore, death no longer mattered. Being already a man marked as past his time, he might do anything, and not worry.

He heard the look-outs yell.

The Number Two started up, looking eager. Wolz continued to sit. He would do all that Kuppisch asked him to do, as a good submariner, but during the attack the skipper and his team were the ones who mattered.

The orders rattled through the boat.

Wolz heard it all as though it was a shadow-play mimed away beyond a gauze curtain. The water bursting into the ballast tanks. The throaty bellow of the diesels cutting at the exact right moment for the electric motors to group in and not suck the boat's air into the diesels. The tilt of the deck. The feel of the boat about him. U-40 handled well, despite the sticky valve on Number Five tank.

At periscope depth they levelled off. A bearded face showed between the curtains of the wardroom. 'Herr Leutnant. Daddy invites you to the control room – if you wish—'

Wolz was in the control room instantly, stuffing himself away inconspicuously, quite consciously thankful to be here and not skulking in the wardroom during an action, although there was nothing he could do. Kuppisch was an old hand – Wolz had looked forward to shipping out with him as much as he had with Ludecke – and this attack would be copy-book stuff up until the single torpedo struck. After that, of course, the hell would start.

All that presupposed that the torpedo functioned correctly.

Kuppisch gave his orders in a flat metallic way, a hard snap to his commands, quite different from the warmer way Ludecke had been wont to bellow out his orders. The men of the attack team knew what they were doing, no doubt of that. The Number One had ignored Wolz – rather oddly, Wolz thought – and his face looked ugly and ridged in the lighting, deeply-bearded, haggard. Wolz could not see his eyes. The Number One was a man called Stoller, and all Wolz had heard of him at base was that he was not much interested in women and to keep your little brothers indoors. In the Nazi circles Wolz knew about he was well aware the risks Stoller ran; what would happen to him if a whisper reached the ears of the S.S., for instance.

From Wolz's viewpoint the attack was carried out in pure text-book fashion. He admired Kuppisch's technique. The heavy thrashing beat of powerful propellers passed. The hydrophone operator called bearings and the periscope went up and down smartly. Kuppisch rapped out courses and speeds and bearings and the attack table spewed back the answers and the gyro of the single remaining torpedo was set. Now the noise of more propellers echoed about them, a sound that seemed to encompass them with all the potential of horror.

Kuppisch brought U-40 skilfully past the screen of the destroyers. With only four escorts the British would probably adopt the diamond formation – one ahead, one each to port and starboard, and a tail-end charlie. Once past the line of the nearest destroyer, the carrier would lie open and vulnerable.

U-40 slid through the sea like a sleek grey wolf.

The express-train roaring of propellers raced away overhead. The director angle had been brought off perfectly by Kuppisch. With the information given him by Wolz he had achieved a bow position and could allow one destroyer to speed away to port and pop up his tube between that one and the carrier.

By the time the stern destroyer was up the eel would be on its way and the U-boat diving for the depths and safety.

The tenseness hung in the boat. It brought out prickles of sweat. The men breathed lightly. The stink of unwashed bodies, the oily atmosphere, the reek of unventilated steel spaces was forgotten. This was the supreme moment. This was what U-boats had been created to do. Now was the moment to justify the U-boat arm of the Kriegsmarine.

Wolz longed to be able to straddle the seat in the

kiosk and peer through the periscope eyepiece. But he was a mere passenger. He watched hungrily as the attack team went through the routine. His hands were gripped into fists. His face looked devilish. And, still, the soggy cigar end gripped between his teeth, forgotten, jutting up arrogantly, gave his taut features that extra dimension of ferocity removed from precise calculation and scientific routine.

The preparatory orders were all given. The tube flooded up and the bow cap opened. The last calculations were fed in.

The split-seconds passed ... Wolz saw the bearded faces of the men, the way they held themselves, the odd rigid angles of their heads ... He could smell, suddenly and with stomach-ridging nausea, the foul stench of the boat wash over him like an effluvium from hell ... The sudden sharp commands as the button was pressed ..

'Loose!'

The boat thumped. Water bubbled to compensate. Kuppisch rapped out his orders in that hard metallic voice. Full right rudder, planes hard a-dive, full revolutions, take her down to the depths, seek to escape the wrath that was about to break over them ...

Wolz was counting to himself. The stopwatches were gripped in sweaty palms. The seconds ticked away.

The sound of the detonation through the water smacked in like sunrise over heaven.

The men reacted. They shouted and cheered and a man clapped Wolz on the shoulder, quite beside himself with joy. Kuppisch restored order with a single curt command. The hydrophone operator was now their link with the outside world.

In a stray shaft of light the Number One's hands showed, and Wolz saw the shake, the tremor, and the way Stoller gripped his hands together into writhing fists, grinding them together, fighting down his fear. Wolz saw that.

'Screw effect approaching fast,' said the hydrophone operator.

They could hear the irregular pulsing thrum above their heads. They passed over, going rapidly. Fourteen feet in one second – that was the speed depth-charges fell through the sea.

The red needles of the depth gauges flickered across the dials. U-40 plunged for the depths. Fifty metres ... Sixty metres ... Seventy metres ...

The four bangs punched at the steel plates of the boat, as though a madman sought to crush the plating between fingers of insanely strong steel. The boat shuddered. The glass of the dials fell out and splintered across the deck. The lights blinked off. Men fell and staggered. Men screamed. The boat righted herself, somehow, twisting through the deep dark waters.

Half-sitting, half-crouched in his corner in the absolute blackness, Wolz felt a heavy mass fall upon him. He was stifled. The stink of cheap scent wafted unpleasantly to his nostrils, quite unlike the expensive perfumes the officers used to counter the smell of the U-boats. He put out a hand and said: 'You all right?'

The man did not answer. Wolz pushed him off and tried to ease him gently to the deck. He felt the wet stickiness on his palms. His probing fingers felt the back of the man's head, the long hair over the overall collar, the soft and spongy edge of bone and the pulsing heat of sticky substances bubbling under his hands. A rivet sprung by the violence of the depth-charges had smashed into the back of the man's head.

Wolz felt the nausea rise from his stomach, and choked, and fought it back. He put the man down.

Blue emergency lighting came on, making ghosts of everyone.

Four more depth-charges cracked away, near, spilling a drift of dust and chips from the overhead. A valve spewed water and the control room P.O. sprang and twisted desperately, shutting off the inflow. Men glared around, like rats, trapped, frightened.

The animal stink of fear permeated the boat.

'Shut that man up!' snapped Kuppisch.

The whimpering mewling ceased.

The boat twisted as Kuppisch rapped out orders. U-40 turned and dived down and still deeper down, and more depth-charges plummeted after her, exploding with incredible violence about her steel hull. In the blue lighting as the boat shook and debris rained down and the men yelled and fought to stay on their feet, Wolz saw the Number One. Stoller stood gripping a valve wheel, frozen, his hands shaking as he gripped. He was unable to control his fear. His face looked dreadful.

Again the depth-charges rained down.

Kuppisch drove the boat hard at full speed on a course at right angles to the destroyer's course. The moment the racket of the depth-charges ceased he ordered: 'Stop both', and the boat drifted. Everyone hung tense, their mouths open, breathing with that heavy harsh effort of men attempting to remain quiet when all they wanted to do was scream and scream and scream.

The blood on the floor plates looked black, slimy and obscene.

A strange brushing knock against the hull made Wolz cock his head.

The noise came back, almost as though someone outside was knocking on the hull with a pin hammer.

Knock – tang – knock – tang ...

'That's no mermaid,' said Kuppisch.

Knock – knock—

And then the knocking speeded up, as though two hammers were in use, beating a staccato rhythm against the steel hull.

'Half ahead both.'

U-40 crept along through the water. The depth needles with the splintered glass faces showed ninety metres. At this depth the water was as hard as iron. The depth-charges could reach out with lethal force for a great distance, driving in the plates of the boat with pile-driver force.

Knock – knock—

Now the knocking resonated, as though a series of gongs was being struck in rapid succession.

'Steer two-six-oh.'

The boat turned. Depth-charges rained down. Once more the boat was shaken as though gripped in gigantic fangs. The lights flickered. Wolz prayed they would not go out. Kuppisch staggered. Wolz saw him grab for the gyro compass and miss and a depth-charge erupted so close that the whole boat was smashed bodily sideways, corkscrewing. Kuppisch fell. His head struck the edge of the gyro compass stand. His white cap flew off. He sprawled to the deck, his arms outflung. Blood, black and gleaming, streamed from his head, pouring over his face.

The Number One, Stoller, screamed.

He was crazed. He began to climb the ladder to the conning tower. The control room P.O. shouted: 'No! No—'

Stoller kicked the P.O. in the face and scrabbled desperately up the steel rungs. He took a grip on the wheel. The quartermaster in the kiosk was shouting. Men were screaming. Water was sloshing about inboard, and no one had reported battle damage.

Wolz stood up.

Stoller could never open the outer hatch against the water pressure; but his example was destroying the boat, destroying the crew's morale. They had abandoned their duty, and the inevitable result of that was death.

Wolz had kept all the twists and turns of the boat in his head as Kuppisch sought to evade the deadly destroyers.

'Steer one-oh-oh. Full ahead both!' bellowed Wolz.

He pushed past the P.O. who was staggering back, groaning, holding his head. He took Stoller about the shins and pulled. He pulled hard. Stoller crashed down but remained upright, holding the ladder still, his hand dripping blood where the steel had gashed in as Wolz pulled.

Wolz hit him flush alongside the jaw.

'P.O.! Take Number One and stow him safely in a corner. Steer oh-four-five. Port motor only. One knot.'

The Chief Engineer responded with a look aimed at Wolz that said, clearly: 'Thank God someone has taken over.'

U-40 turned and slowed and drifted.

Knock – knock—

Wolz felt his stomach as a single ball of fire, burning him. He wanted to be sick. The enclosed place with its insane mass of piping and valves, the closeness of it, like a tunnel in hell, abruptly pressed in on him. He had never been bothered by the claustrophobia of a U-boat. He knew every pipe, every valve, every gauge, every switch. Yet they appeared to writhe together, closing in, pressing on him. He opened his mouth and dragged in air, tasting the metallic flatness, the staleness of it, the oil and scent and water—

'Damage control report! Fore ends?'

The phone spat and then the words came through: 'Taking water. Slow leak. I'm plugging now—'

'Engine room?'

The phone crackled. 'All right here. But the starboard motor's hot. A bearing going—'

'Run it until it burns! I'll tell you when to switch off.'

'Very good!'

The water seeping into the fore ends presented a problem. If that seawater found the batteries and the acid – chlorine gas would do for the U-boat's crew what the English destroyers had so far failed to do.

The knocking ghosted against the steel hull. The

pinging sounds drifted and came back, vanished, returned, vanished again.

Wolz checked the depth gauges.

Over ninety metres.

The knocking had stopped.

The men looked at him in the blue light, like ghouls, like vampires wanting to suck his blood. Their eyes were deeply sunk into their heads. Their faces were pebbly, grained with fear. Wolz listened.

The beat of the destroyers' propellers was there, but faint and growing fainter.

'What is the bearing now?'

'Propeller effect bearing two-seven-oh, receding,' said the hydrophone operator.

The boat stank. The water was running into the fore ends, dripping down the deck past the metal, running down to collect in the battery spaces below. There was precious little time left. The knocking had stopped. Wolz had deduced what the men had not understood. The boat had dropped below her ninety metres because she'd blundered into an area of fresher water in the sea. He fancied that sheet of heavier water had acted like a mirror, or perhaps a sponge – he didn't know – and had fooled whatever the English were using to knock on his hull. The destroyers were pulling away. The screw noises faded.

He took a breath, feeling dizzy.

Stoller slumbered. The Commander groaned and rolled onto his side. The bandage they'd wrapped about his head was already stained. The control room P.O., recovered, was putting in fresh bulbs. The lighting came on. The Chief stood up and started to check out his circuits. The planesmen concentrated on their wheels and gauges.

'Blow main ballast, Chief,' said Wolz. 'Periscope depth.'

U-40, still alive, began to rise through the dark water which was her home.

That night U-40 limped slowly northward on the surface.

The dead had been buried with due honours. A madman lay writhing and shrieking against his gag, strapped down on a bunk in the wardroom. Leutnant zur See Baldur Wolz had taken over as Number One. Kapitanleutnant Otto Kuppisch, wearing his bandage at a rakish angle, had resumed command. The memory of Ludecke gave Wolz feelings he could not completely analyse.

No-one had heard any breaking-up sounds after their torpedo had exploded. It had struck. There was no doubt of that. They would claim a hit on *Ark Royal* and Donitz would be pleased. But whether or not they had sunk her – Wolz put his mind to the matters that would concern him most immediately on this long haul home – they had done all they could with the weapons given them.

This ending to the patrol, now. They would have to sail north around Scotland. But they would do it. Wolz felt that most strongly. They were sailing home across the sea .

His thoughts encompassed many things and many people. He was sailing home to romps with Lottie and Heidi. He would see his cousins again and no doubt Marlene would sing and dance. He would see Trudi. The shiver of premonition as he thought of her felt delicious, delicious and dangerous. He would not think of his cousin Lisl.

The Third Reich demanded a great deal of all its citizens and much more of its fighting men. Of all those men fighting for Adolf Hitler and the Nazis and the Third Reich, perhaps none dared so much and ran so many dangers and struck more shrewd blows than the men of the U-boat service.

Baldur Wolz sailed home to Germany. He was realistic enough to know that, despite all he had done, he would not receive command of his own boat as yet.

He would go out on patrol again. That was certain. Once more he would take a boat out into the hostile sea and drive that slender steel hull through the waves and try to sink the enemy.

Again and again he would go out on patrol. That was his future.

His destiny lay with the U-boats.

His destiny until the day he died.

A selection of Bestsellers from Sphere Books

TEMPLE DOGS	Robert L. Duncan	95p	☐
THE PASSAGE	Bruce Nicolayson	95p	☐
CHARLIE IS MY DARLING	Mollie Hardwick	£1.25p	☐
RAISE THE TITANIC!	Clive Cussler	95p	☐
KRAMER'S WAR	Derek Robinson	£1.25p	☐
THE CRASH OF '79	Paul Erdman	£1.25p	☐
EMMA AND I	Sheila Hocken	85p	☐
UNTIL THE COLOURS FADE	Tim Jeal	£1.50p	☐
DR. JOLLY'S BOOK OF CHILDCARE			
	Dr. Hugh Jolly	£1.95p	☐
MAJESTY	Robert Lacey	£1.50p	☐
STAR WARS	George Lucas	95p	☐
FALSTAFF	Robert Nye	£1.50p	☐
EXIT SHERLOCK HOLMES	Robert Lee Hall	95p	☐
THE MITTENWALD SYNDICATE			
	Frederick Nolan	95p	☐
CLOSE ENCOUNTERS OF THE THIRD KIND			
	Steven Spielberg	85p	☐
STAR FIRE	Ingo Swann	£1.25p	☐
RUIN FROM THE AIR			
	Gordon Thomas & Max Morgan Witts	£1.50p	☐
EBANO (Now filmed as ASHANTI)			
	Alberto Vazquez-Figueroa	95p	☐
FIREFOX	Craig Thomas	95p	☐

All Sphere books are available at your local bookshop or newsagent, or can be ordered direct from the publisher. Just tick the titles you want and fill in the form below.

Name..

Address..

....

Write to Sphere Books, Cash Sales Department, P.O. Box 11, Falmouth, Cornwall TR10 9EN

Please enclose cheque or postal order to the value of the cover price plus:

UK: 22p for the first book plus 10p per copy for each additional book ordered to a maximum charge of 82p

OVERSEAS: 30p for the first book and 10p for each additional book

BFPO & EIRE: 22p for the first book plus 10p per copy for the next 6 books, thereafter 4p per book

Sphere Books reserve the right to show new retail prices on covers which may differ from those previously advertised in the text or elsewhere, and to increase postal rates in accordance with the GPO.

(12:78)